Introduction

How short is a short story? We know it's less than a novel but how short can it be? Is the thing that distinguishes it something to do with its length, or is it something else? Are these important questions in determining what constitutes a short story?

Let's begin with what it is not. A short story is not an edited down novel. Nor is it a poem. It is not a section or a chapter of a longer work. It is something that should satisfy on its own terms. It needs to have a sense of completion. Wholeness. Something realised. A finished article. So what is it that produces this feeling? For me it is principally to do with focus.

In this world of the short story, you don't have a great deal of time or space. You're in a limited universe. You need to get to the heart of things quite quickly. You don't have the luxury of a large canvas. You have to tell your tale through a detail. In that detail, all of the world that you need to create, must be present and revealed. It is a tall order and a difficult task.

Many aspiring writers are drawn to the short form because they think it is easier than taking on a novel. In many ways, it is more difficult. For it requires the courage and skill of a surgeon to be able to cut through to the bone. To pare away the flesh, to discard excess, to look for the essence, the atom, the molecule. Patrick Kavanagh described it perfectly when he said that 'the secret is in the crumb.'

The stories in this collection have many of the elements required for good short story writing. They have humour, irony and best of all, anarchy. Nothing kills our interest more than predictability. Readers crave surprise, shock, edginess, attitude and above all, insight. A glass of wine spills on a table and makes a strange shape that looks like a map of Spain; an aspiring young artist enters a competition but meets a woman who may turn out to be a bigger prize; a woman starts a course only to discover that she's been sitting on one buttock for twenty years. These are crisp and telling observations that stimulate our interest and make us want to read on. They are just some of the elements in this thought provoking, entertaining and incisive collection of stories. It is heartening to see so many writers honing their craft in this deceptively difficult medium.

Peter Sheridan

Dublin Stories

THE SIXTH COLLECTION

Dedicated To Donal Twomey

Introduced by: Peter Sheridan

An Inkwell Publication

2005

An Inkwell Publication
2005

Inkwell is the publishing mark of the
Inkwell Writers Group Dublin

© 2005 Inkwell

Set in Ehrhardt 11/13
Typesetting and Design: M & J Graphics

Printing: Future Print Ltd, Dubllin

British cataloguing in Publications Data
A catalogue record for this book is available from the British Library

ISBN 0 9529462 6 2

Cover illustration: Danny Skehan

Contents

The Retro Feminists

Breda Nathan

'Down with men. We would all be virgins only for them.'

Maybe I should have walked out then. It was my first night at the Assertiveness for Women class. I was trying to change my behaviour from passive to a 'moving forward' type of woman, returning to work after rearing my two sons. I told my mother I was joining the ICA.

I had secured a job through my best friend Laura, who was sleeping with the boss, Hugo, but I had made a pretty dismal start. Both my husband and my mother were totally against my returning to work and my friendship with Laura. If they knew the full story, they would have had my children placed for adoption. Not even Laura knew I was taking the lessons, it was going to be my secret.

The course tutor discovered I was sitting on one buttock for twenty years, in the 'compassion trap', it's called. It's a psycho-social legacy, defined as a sense of obligation felt by women, who put everyone else's needs before their own and are always accessible. This is usually passed on from mother to daughter; in my case, probably my grandmother, my mother being a very capable woman.

While I was inadequate in many ways, this did not seem to apply to my fellow students. There were two separated Sandras, a small and a very large Elaine, (the larger having an affair) a divorced

1

Dolores and June, who was considering a sexual fling with another woman. My mother's face was flashing like a beacon before me. I was the only 'still married' person there. It felt so ordinary.

Trying to put my new skills into action next evening, I ignored the doorbell. That didn't work. The knocker echoed through the house. I peeped out. It was Laura. I was almost pleased. Here was my chance to try the new assertive me. I partly opened the door. She looked at me strangely and pushed, I kept my foot behind it.

'I'm busy tonight, Laura,' I said, 'I can allow you ten minutes of my time.' I looked at my watch sternly, like the tutor does.

'Feck off Mary,' she said, brushing past me and plugging in the kettle. 'I have some good news for you.' I got the coffee jar. Obviously I was not yet ready for power dressing.

'Germaine Greer is coming to Dublin. I got two tickets for her lecture in UCD,' she said. I made the mistake of confiding in her then. I told her all about the assertiveness participants and how I hoped to become more focused and not allow myself to be used. She was supportive in her own way.

'This lecture is just what you need, Mary. We can reclaim our days as revolutionaries. Have you a bottle of wine there?'

That was the end of my study for that night. It doesn't matter now I suppose, but sometimes I still wonder why everyone knows better than me what I want or need.

The second meeting of the assertiveness group was a sort of role-play, where you have to deal with a 'situation'. I'm never good in situations, so I should have had an expectation of trouble, of course I didn't.

We had to separate into twos. Unfortunately, June was my partner. You had to imagine you were in a type of courtroom, trying to argue a case for your rights after being betrayed by a man. My story was short and to the point.

'I feel I am not being appreciated,' I started. 'My husband and sons take me for granted. I would like to get a proper job and have some independence.'

'Get a grip,' she screamed. 'You are not living in the real world.'

I was sort of stuttering about my rights, but she dismissed them out of hand. I could have said several things I only thought of later. I should have said it was people like her who had given me a stutter, but I just allowed her to launch into a diatribe. God almighty would not argue with that woman.

There was a tirade of abuse against her many former partners, we were not allowed to say husband or wife, it was all partner and longtime friend. You just listened, if you were clever. That's when she casually mentioned she was considering this fling with a woman after years of failed relationships with men. Maybe I was a tad tactless, but we were supposed to be honest. It's the way her jaw juts out though.

'Don't you feel you're a bit of a pervert?' I asked politely. As I spoke, I knew it was a mistake. Her colour changed several times. The tutor explained it to me later, while she was reviving me. Apparently she experienced frustration and anger and came down on the side of anger. You should remember not to grit your teeth. This lessens the conviction in your statement. June ignored this. I saw the tension in her big jaw. You see assertion slips easily into aggression and the body language becomes hostile and threatening. She allowed it to, and gave me a bang of her umbrella. Something went against my breath and I tripped over my bag. I grabbed the tutor by the chest and we hit the floor running.

The tutor suggested I move to another table. They were starting a quilt group. I thought in my innocence it might be relaxing, before they mentioned the Celtic designs and gave me a red square to complete in some intricate lacey pattern. I was never much use at knitting or sewing at school, so I knew I would have problems. I remembered trying to turn a heel of a mauve sock for about five years, without success. When I told Laura about this, she recommended I rob one of her mother's doilies.

'It has to be red,' I answered foolishly.

'Put it in the washing machine with a lump of beetroot,' she said. She's so artistic.

On Saturday I told my mother I was going to a conference in

UCD. It sounded intellectual so she agreed to cook dinner for the family. When we arrived in Belfield I was nearly relaxed. The hall was packed and we had to take separate seats. Would you believe my bad luck? I sat down next to June. I was raging. I didn't want to get into a conversation about perverts again.

'Hi Mary. I'm surprised to see you here,' she said, friendly enough. 'I wouldn't have thought of you as a radical woman.'

'Oh really?' I was very quick this time. 'As a matter of fact I would have been seen as a revolutionary in the seventies.'

'No.'

'Yes. And what's more, I did a lot of work for a very ... at that time, extremist organisation.'

'Who?'

'The Maoists. I often stayed up all night printing material for them, with stencils. There were no computers then.

'Well that would have been before my time. I thought you were going to tell me you were on the condom train with Nell McCafferty or Mary Kenny. You know there were more people on that train than in the GPO in 1916'

'Is that right?' I answered. 'Were you in the GPO?'

She didn't reply. I made a point of sitting flat down and checked the two hundred women and fifteen men in the lecture hall. About eighty per cent of them were sitting on one buttock.

Germaine is a marvelous woman. To have stayed in that frame of mind for a lifetime, is quite amazing. Some of her statements were a bit...well a bit strong. I didn't say this to Laura, but I had sort of grown out of that way of thinking. And I found some of the stuff crude. Maybe I am going like my mother. I kept thinking that I wouldn't like my kids to be listening. You know the stuff you thought brilliant when you were young, stuff that you have kind of grown out of. I suppose I have conformed. It's sad when you think of it. Some of it is still valid in today's world, but when she shouted things like 'So you can piss standing up' or 'I hope feminism is about destroying society' I cringed. My doubts about entering June's real world were increasing. I was more disturbed than stimulated coming out.

We went for a drink with Laura's old neighbour, Grace. They were sitting beside each other at the front of the hall. Laura hadn't seen her for years actually, since she accused Grace of trying to poison her new boyfriend. When I reminded her of this, she brushed it off and said Grace was off her medication at the time. I didn't question that. Whether she was back on her medication I'm not sure, but they were both definitely restored to full radicalism. We had bought Germaine's book and had it signed. I was reading bits while we waited to be served. Laura was agog with new words and reclaimed feminism. I just couldn't get into the spirit of it.

'What did you think, Mary?' She didn't give me time to answer. The power was almost dripping out of her mouth.

'Wasn't she great?'

'Yeah, though I think ...'

'When you realise the bastards men are. I'll tell you one thing Mary, that hoor, Hugo, is in for a shock.'

'Well I'm not sure you should do anything hasty, Laura.'

'I'm not being hasty. I've allowed him to rule my life, probably ruin my life.'

'He didn't put a gun to your head, Laura.' Maybe for a minute I was thinking of my own job. Honest to God I don't know.

'He controlled me and urged me to conform to patriarchy. I was never that type. You know I wasn't.' She turned to Grace.

'Do you see deterioration in me, Grace?' Of course Grace could see it clearly and we were only on our first drink.

Worse was to come. Large Elaine arrived in with one of the Sandras and sat at the next table. I didn't want to introduce them. You know the way people like that don't mix and I was the connection. I was trying to smile at them behind Laura and Grace's back but Sandra came over.

'Would your friends be interested in joining our quilt group?'

I nearly died. I was thinking of the Celtic designs and Laura's lump of beetroot plan. Within five minutes Laura and Grace had been signed up. Laura was talking like she was born and bred in the heart of Carrickmacross. If I was a poor example from our domestic science class, Laura was a dead loss altogether, but to listen to her, you would think she was one of those craft knitters with a needle never out of her hand. I don't know where she gets the nerve.

By the time we had our fourth round, Laura had taken over the quilt and she was planning embroidered messages of death threats to all men, on scalloped edgings. She hadn't even met June. I kept looking around to see who was listening. I couldn't even get merry, with my nerves.

'Laura,' I started. 'I don't think it would be a good idea for you to get too involved in this quilt business, after all you are very busy.'

'I am never too busy to help my sisters in their hour of need (sniff).' She was starting to dribble.

'I will be the first to reclaim...reclaim my...everything...'

'It will be difficult to reclaim your virginity Laura.'

'I am very dish ... Dishappointed in you Mary. I think that was uncalled for.'

I ran up to the bar and ordered another brandy. Large Elaine was making a speech when I came back.

'I think these gatherings are great for meeting people of like minds. I'm delighted to meet you, Laura.'

She was only short of kissing her.

'That's what it's all about Elaine,' Laura said. 'Networking, we must be available to look out for our sisters. We must never be in the position of our poor mothers. I watched my mother rub the skin off her fingers on a wash board, while my father sat drinking in the local bar.'

'Laura, your mother was a school principal. She had a cleaning lady. Your father was the bank manager. They didn't drink.'

'Well it must have been my grandmother. Shut up Mary, these stories must be passed down from generation to generation. We must redefine feminism for a new generation.'

I'd had enough. What was I doing here? More stressed than I

ever was, as a stay-at-home-mum. I made a quick phone call home,

'Mammy, you were right,' I said, 'I have decided to give up my job. Tell them all, I'll be home soon.' She was delighted.

'I'll have your hot chocolate ready, darling,' she answered. Thank heavens I never told them about the course or the women's lib. lecture, I thought happily.

It was twelve o'clock when I got them out of the pub. The taxi man insisted on going to my house first. When we arrived at our gate, my mother was at the door waiting. I was trying to straighten myself up getting out of the car, but just as the driver was pulling away Laura put her head out the window and roared.

'DON'T FORGET, MARY. THE PENIS IS A WEAPON.'

A Sister's Position

Paddy Ryan

'Your poor brother died a hero,' an overweight blonde woman, whose name Bríd Cooney is unable to place, extends a pudgy hand in sympathy. Bríd responds mechanically as she follows her parents to the mourning car. Glancing at the sea of faces, she realizes that Pádraig's death when the bomb he was carrying exploded at Paddington Station, is the most newsworthy event for years in this small north Cork town.

Busying herself with the red beret perched on her coiled, black hair, Bríd feels like shouting that this spectacle would not be taking place if only she'd responded to her brother's call. But she lied about working late because she couldn't wait to see Trevor who was returning from Glasgow. She now knows that was Pádraig's call for help and she failed him.

'I hope the burial is over before the rain,' her father says as she gets in the car. 'I'd hate to see the people get wet.' The concentration on his face when he leans forward to look at the two men in balaclavas arranging the tricolour over Pádraig's coffin, disturbs her. Wishing she did not blame him for what's happened, she turns to watch a pile of pink and purple confetti swirling in the strong April breeze.

Bríd has often imagined standing with Trevor at this church for their wedding photographs. But Pádraig's bomb splintered that dream like it killed the Indian cleaner and a young Dutch backpacker. She recalls her First Communion photo here on the church steps. But she recalls more vividly how sick she'd felt worrying about her father who'd been taken away by the Guards the previous evening.

'It's only politics, love. You wait and see; he'll be home before night,' her mother had tried to soothe her. Although he was home that evening, it was too late for the trip to the city.

'Where are your gloves?' her mother asks, massaging Bríd's knuckles, 'your hands are blue.'

'The sign of a good nurse,' she murmurs but she wants to say that her bones have been blocks of ice since identifying Pádraig's mangled body for the London police. There was also the blazing row with Trevor when she refused to let him accompany her. And now it strikes her that this scene will be relayed into Penton Mewsey, the Hampshire village where Trevor's parents live. She wants to give them a reassuring wave, a signal that she does not share her dead brother's politics.

'There's that Mr Horkan who taught Pádraig in sixth class,' her mother says.

'He never liked him,' her father growls, glaring at the middle-aged man huddled in a navy overcoat, 'And the way he put his own spin on the '98 rebellion and the Rising. Little respect for them that gave their lives for Ireland.'

'Maybe he was right,' Bríd murmurs and steadily holds her father's angry gaze as the car edges out behind the hearse and down the market square.

'Why is he being buried in Kilthubber rather than here in town?' she asks.

'He's being laid to rest with his own,' her father says. And Bríd recalls the large Celtic cross, the base carved with round towers and shamrock, over his grandfather in Kilthubber. Every time they'd visited it, he told them about the October evening when black and tans shot the young man, standing with his little daughter at the door. For years, she thought he'd also been present; the details were so graphic.

'They could draw the blinds when a worker's funeral is

passing,' he says as the funeral halts before a building with Solo Systems in large blue letters over the doors. Assembling computer parts in this factory must have given Pádraig the notion that he could make bombs, she thinks.

'Typical Americans,' her mother agrees, 'profit and more profits.' Bríd looks at the cars parked in front of the building, around which beds of velvet brown wallflowers and vivid blue pansies are braving the breeze. A weeping willow near the gates reminds her of the water meadows that were here when she was a child. And she realizes that it's been over two years since she was last home.

'People were saying you're getting very like Aunt Nell,' her mother murmurs, 'the same brown eyes and pale skin.' Recalling a letter telling of Nell's death, she vaguely notes the farmhouses, haybarns and upland fields flashing past as if she was watching a familiar movie being replayed over and over.

'The television boys are here before us,' she's brought back to the present with their driver's high-pitched voice as he slows to a halt. Her anger bubbles, deciding that her father has reneged on his promise of no military trappings, when he hurries out and over to the hearse. Linking her mother, Bríd wipes the tears as she looks down into the open grave under the Celtic cross. When she lifts her head, it strikes her that the little church has a twin in Penton Mewsey. She feels there is something meaningful, even profound, about that similarity but she is too numbed to figure it out. Lifting her eyes, she shivers seeing the rooks silent and vulture-like in the leafless belt of trees and beyond them the black hills unsoftened yet by Spring.

'All he's missing is a pair of runners and a track suit,' her father mutters when the young priest quickly starts the prayers. As her grip tightens on his arm, Bríd is surprised when she realizes that his heavy frame is actually shivering. But then, like a spring uncoiled, he shakes free, nearly tripping in his hurry to help remove the tricolour from Pádraig's coffin. Carefully folding it, he seems oblivious to the crowd, the cameras or the Gardaí. A single shot echoes and the smile that briefly creases his face disappears as the priest shuts his prayer book and, without a word, walks quickly to the gate.

'Pádraig kept the rain away until it finished,' he says when they are back in the car and the drops plop against the windscreen. Putting an arm around her mother who is sobbing, Bríd recalls his story about two brothers who were hanged in the market square for the alleged murder of a landlord. The executions were hardly over when flashes of fork lightning lit the July sky that had inexplicably darkened. He'd claimed the hangings took place where her mother and himself set up stall to sell Easter lilies. And each year Pádraig had eagerly looked forward to standing with them, ever hopeful of increasing sales. From an early age, despite her father's pleas, she had refused to accompany them, hating the looks on neighbours' faces as they studiously avoided them. She had secretly prayed that her parents could be more like everybody else's father and mother.

'Do you have to leave soon?' her mother asks as they approach the town.

'The sooner, the better,' Bríd retorts.

Her father glares at her to keep quiet, pointing at the driver. The nagging feeling that he encouraged Pádraig to his death flashes across her brain with fresh urgency. And fragmented memories of the sturdy, red-haired child, who tried so hard to please his parents, keep floating in her head like a jigsaw that will not fit.

An ambulance with flashing lights reminds Bríd of her father's opposition to her going to England after she'd failed to secure a place in an Irish hospital. But anxious to get away, she'd gone ahead without his approval. A few nights before she left for London, she was surprised to overhear him boast to that fellow from Belfast who was staying with them:

'I'm glad one of mine will get something from England, after all they took from us.'

She only realizes they are home in Plunkett Park when another battery of silvery flashes envelopes them and reporters push mikes at them. Noticing her father's hesitancy, she gently pushes him towards the door where her Aunt Una is shouting about privacy.

'I was proud of ye on the news,' she says when they are inside, 'so dignified, especially you, Bríd, considering the ordeal you had to go through in London.'

It's as if the last week never happened, Bríd thinks, looking at the sittingroom wallpaper, the painting of Kilthubber cemetery and Pádraig's First Communion photograph. We all looked so forlorn, she thinks and recalls the trip to Dublin, the meal in a hotel and the tour of the jail where the heroes of the Rising were executed. She remembers that the picture was taken outside the prison after the graphic account of the executions had made Pádraig bawl loudly while she, two years older, struggled to hold back the tears. And how her father had to be dragged away from the guide whose information he was to repeat over and over on the journey home

'Pádraig died for his beliefs and him only gone twenty-five, the bed of heaven to him,' Aunt Una crosses herself.

Bríd remains silent and stares intently at the turquoise carpet with its convoluted mossy green designs from the Book of Kells. And she thinks that young men similar to Pádraig, in Palestine and elsewhere, leave homes every day to further causes for which they are prepared to die. But does it give them the right to destroy innocent lives, she asks herself and thinks of the gentle Indian couple who lived next door in Highbury. Everything I've worked so hard for is as nothing now, she thinks furiously.

'Have either of you considered my position?' she asks as her mother lays the cups. 'How can I return to Queen Adelaide's to be called the bomber's sister?'

'You'll get a job in any hospital in this country,' her mother says, 'they're bringing in nurses from the Philippines and other places. You're all we have, now that Pádraig is,' and she hesitates before saying softly, 'that Pádraig is gone.'

Trying to keep her anger down, Bríd replies quietly: 'But I've been happy at Queen Adelaides. And I'm recommended for a

Sister's position. A Sister's position,' she repeats and her hollow laugh echoes in the small, cluttered room.

'That's great,' her mother says, 'I'll get last Sunday's Independent and you'll see all the vacancies, especially for someone with your qualifications,' and she hurries out.

Maybe my duty is to stay and be near them, she thinks and looks down again at the carpet as if the solution to her dilemma lies in the intricate designs.

Lighting a cigarette, she watches the flaming match getting steadier in her hand.

'I wish you wouldn't smoke in this house,' her father says. 'Of all people, you must know the dangers of tobacco.'

'Sorry,' she says, 'I'll take it upstairs.'

Standing at the bedroom window, Bríd looks out on the green where the grass has been pounded to brown earth by the constant football. She sees the years ahead in this house where ideas not conforming to her parents' politics will also be pounded relentlessly, in case there's ever a doubt about Pádraig's status as a hero. And she also realizes that she'll never be sure whether her meeting him that evening in Oxford Street would have changed anything.

She turns to look around the room that had seemed so secure when she woke at night to the comforting snores of her father and her mother's exasperated whispers to sleep on his side. But the wallpaper festooned with yellow roses and the heavy double wardrobes now seem poised to hem her in.

'I have to get away,' she thinks, opening the window and stubbing the cigarette on the sill. With a sweep of an arm, Bríd bundles her belongings from the dressing table and stuffs them with her clothes into the large, black sports bag. And the thick, steel teeth of the sturdy zipper echo off the faded wallpaper long after the door closes behind her.

All That Glitters…

Ann Rhodes

I ignored the phone, just as I was ignoring the insistent figures on the spreadsheet before me. On the screen I saw, not figures and formulas, but a shiny red hull and a tall, strong mast just begging for red sails. Tom McGrane was selling 'Princess Maro' and I'd walked past her for three weeks before I'd finally succumbed yesterday and climbed aboard for a look around. She was beautiful, just what we'd always promised ourselves. Retire when we reached 55, replace the dinghy with a proper boat and set sail. Not around the world or anything daft like that; just around Ireland and maybe the Scottish islands we loved so much. I sighed, remembering the texture of the tiller in my hand and the burnished wood of the cabin. McGrane had made me a coffee and told me he'd be sorry to lose her but he wanted to venture further and needed a bigger boat. He'd had no offers, he told me and I'd asked him what he'd take for her. The lovely red hull on the screen melted into the figures in my projected budget. Alison still had another year at Trinity and Matthew had just begun his PhD at Oxford. I sighed again, this time despairingly. Matthew looked set for a career as a permanent academic, Alison was already talking about a Masters and my fifty-fifth birthday was fast approaching.

'Alan! Are ye deaf? It's for you.' My wife's annoyance at being dragged away from her gardening was obvious and she'd disappeared through the back door before I reached the phone on the kitchen wall. I didn't recognise the English accent that politely asked if I had a cousin called Jeff from Leeds who came to stay every summer. It was when he asked me if I ever got the boat that I knew him. Jeff, whose emigrant mother sent him to her sister every summer for fresh sea air and a bit of the Irish language. We got plenty of fresh air but divil a bit of the Irish language he ever learned. I used to help him to memorise a few phrases before he went home just to please his mother who, never having been to Dublin, thought Ringsend was like the Clare village she grew up in. I pulled a kitchen chair close to the phone and we talked as if forty summers had not filtered through the lanes and meadows we had played in. He'd been clearing out his mother's house, he told me, and he'd found a box in the attic, his childhood treasure box, did I remember? I laughed and told him mine must be lying around somewhere too, full of useless trinkets, shells and shiny pebbles. He still came to Ireland in summer, he said, and we arranged to meet next time he was in town.

He came every May. Da met him off the mail boat and Ma fussed about him, unpacking his battered suitcase and asking him what he'd like to eat. 'Tell her you'd like chips every day,' I told him and when he did I got a clip around the ear. I'd no brothers, only two older sisters who thought I was nothing but a nuisance, so I loved having Jeff around for the whole summer. That first year I took him to all my haunts. Soon he knew how to outrun the tides at Sandymount, climb the Scalp, jump from the high diving board at Blackrock Baths, cook beans over a camp fire in the Pine Forest and sing a rousing chorus of The Wild Rover. My pals loved him, loved his fearlessness and his strange way of talking. By September, his Leeds vocabulary was usually fairly spiced with Dublin phrases and we hated the morning we waved him off home on the mail boat.

That first summer we had a midnight feast the night before he left, creeping out the back door, cycling to Seapoint, the two of us sitting by the Martello tower eating our makeshift banana sandwiches liberally sprinkled with sugar. It was a beautiful night, I remember, with a warm crescent moon and a high tide. We listened to the quiet waves steal up the steps and I envied Jeff his voyage. I loved the sea even then. When the tide reached the top step, Jeff said we should make a wish because his Ma had told him that the sea gods could grant wishes. I wished for a boat with red sails and Jeff wished for a dog.

'Me Mam don't like them,' he told me when I looked surprised. We feasted and repeated those wishes every September until the last summer, the year that Jeff turned sixteen and went to work in a Leeds factory and I started my apprenticeship in the E.S.B.

Great Aunt Kit's house was our favourite place. Every Friday Ma sent us there with a gift of freshly baked soda bread and last week's *Woman's Way*. We didn't want baskets on our handlebars so we took turns to carry Da's green canvas rucksack as we cycled out the coast road. 'That oul wan is rolling in money,' Da used to say with a wink, 'look after her and she might remember yis in the Will!' We didn't believe him for if she had money, her big house in Seapoint wouldn't be so shabby and empty. The lovely old house was indeed derelict except for the few rooms she used but her garden was a wonderland where she grew herbs, strange grasses and beautiful flowers with names we could never remember. At the bottom of the garden, almost at the sea wall, she had an uncultivated patch, her wild garden, she told us, often pointing out the bluebells, roses, violets, primroses and her precious wild orchids that bloomed and melted there throughout the seasons. In a hidden corner she showed us her favourite, not yet ready, but when it was she would harvest it and use it to roll her own cigarettes. That, she said, was just between the three of us and her eyes sparkled like the summer sea when she smiled as we shook hands on our secret.

Great Aunt Kit's fortune was reputed to be a collection of precious jewellery mysteriously acquired by an Elizabethan ancestor and secretly handed down to each generation. I never managed to work out her relationship to us but Da said she was from a different branch of the family but that as she was the last in her line, she'd have to leave the jewels to one of us. We didn't believe that either because she never wore any jewellery and we just couldn't imagine her wearing diamonds as she dug out the flowerbeds each Autumn.

'She's nearly ninety now, ye know,' Da would tease us as we pulled our bikes from behind the shed where Ma kept the wringer. Strange that she never seemed old to us as she worked in her garden, grass-stained skirt hugging her ankles and a battered straw hat jammed over her grey hair. We thought my Mam and Dad were old, but not Great Aunt Kit.

During Jeff's second summer, she gave each of us an identical small wooden box to store our summer hordes. Our treasure boxes. They were old, she told us, the sort of box that ships' captains had used to store their log books during long voyages to new lands. They were strong and the lead lining meant that the contents were safe from the ravages of seawater. Jeff loved to find coloured pebbles and he'd polish them until they shone. I collected shells from the beach and especially loved to scavenge after a storm when I knew that the shells flung to shore were from the deep and were somehow more magical. We only kept the best of our collections, carefully laying them in the boxes. At summer's end, Great Aunt Kit would solemnly lock the boxes with one of the keys she kept on a metal ring in the kitchen. We felt instinctively that the treasure boxes were part of our secret so we didn't want to take them home. We left them each September in her care.

It was during the summer when Da said she was nearly ninety, that we found out about the secret compartment in the treasure boxes. We sat in the afternoon sunshine, one of us on either side of Great Aunt Kit on the old wooden seat near where the honeysuckle crawled along the trellis. Our treasure hordes lay in a pile on the grass as we held our breath and watched. Carefully she unlocked each box's secret in turn, laying them upside down and tracing the faint pattern I had never noticed before. When I peered closely at it I saw a Viking longboat with oarsmen straining against the waves. Using the tiniest key we had ever seen, she tapped the second oarsman's head twice and slotted the key between the oar and the boat. With an almost silent click, a tiny drawer slid from beneath the Viking long boat.

'…for the extra special treasure you might one day find,' she said and lit one of her cigarettes, inhaling deeply, 'but you have to hit the right spot'. We practised all summer and although it took us a while, we managed to master the secret lock before Jeff left for Leeds. The summer had not yielded any special treasure so the secret compartments remained empty. We didn't mind. We returned the tiny key to Great Aunt Kit who put it on a piece of string around her neck, and we hugged the secret to ourselves.

The following summer Great Aunt Kit died. She had fallen ill during the uncertain Spring that had followed a long, cold winter. Her garden lay unattended and we tried unsuccessfully to tend to it, following the instructions she issued from within the mound of pillows that were now her world. Now, Mam came with us sometimes to tend to our old friend and as the summer crept damply towards Autumn, other people came to visit too, people we had never seen before. 'Gold diggers!' I heard Da hiss one night when Ma told him who had been. He never visited her at all. We still kept our treasure boxes under Great Aunt Kit's kitchen sink but without the key we could not open the secret drawers. '..t'aint as if there's owt in 'em secret bits,' Jeff pointed out and in truth we had added precious little to our treasure that dreary summer.

A Friday night knock at our back door brought the news that Great Aunt Kit was going downhill fast. Family members had descended on the old house, gathering about her bed to pray but she had waved them to silence and asked that the boys be brought to her. Ma and Da argued about letting us go and when we said we'd like to see our old friend again, they relented and all four of us got the bus to Seapoint in the rain. A tall gentleman wearing a dark suit seemed to be in charge at the house. Two women who stood smoking near the honeysuckle, glared at us as he ushered us in from the rain. There seemed to be people all over the house and they all seemed to be glaring at the tall gentleman or at us.

'You are good boys to come,' he said loudly, 'your aunt is very fond of you both.' He winked at us and oblivious to the frisson of resentment that rippled through the decaying hall, led us upstairs. The bright bedroom with the window always open to the summer air, where we three had played cards, talked, rolled Great Aunt Kit's cigarettes and received our gardening instructions was now shrouded in gloom. We hesitated at the door as we surveyed the scene, window tightly shut, dark curtains we had never noticed before firmly drawn and the only source of light coming from two tall black candles firmly ensconced in heavy gilt candlesticks that were taller than me and Jeff. People we didn't know sat solemnly about the room and four women who were kneeling reverently by the bed ceased their murmuring when we stepped into the room. We were quite scared now but the tall man and Ma and Da were behind us in the doorway and there was nothing for it but to advance quietly into the room. We crept close to the bed and stood nervously by the candlestick. Great Aunt Kit was curled up beneath a mountain of blankets with not even her head peeping out. We tried not to grin but we both remembered her saying she slept like that so she could jump out and frighten burglars. How I wished she'd jump out and get rid of all the people in the room. Behind us the chant of prayer began again and under its cover I whispered to her. After a few minutes, the shape beneath the blankets seemed to stretch. A long thin arm reached out, a hand-rolled cigarette expertly pinched between two fingers. Slowly the arm reached upward, guiding the cigarette towards the flickering black candle-light. Behind us there was a stunned silence as all eyes were on the cigarette blooming rosily to life. They were too engrossed to notice her other hand dart forward to slip a tiny key into my hand. Beneath her nest of blankets, Great Aunt Kit winked cheerily at us before drawing deeply on the cigarette, sending rings of sweet smoke to lighten the gloom.

In the end, she had the last laugh but probably not as loud as Da when he heard that she'd had the jewellery right enough, genuine Elizabethan stuff. She'd already sold it and she left the money to a woodland trust charity out beyond Glenmalure. The old house was to be sold and the proceeds were to be used to set up a public wild garden near the sea. She'd left the two treasure boxes to us though – a wooden box and all its contents – to each of us. The tall gentleman had delivered mine to me just before Christmas that year and he told me that Jeff's had been sent to him in Leeds.

'Full of junk' my sisters said scornfully but they rummaged through just in case. We had pledged not to open the secret drawers until we were together again, and anyway I had given the key to Jeff for safe keeping away from my sisters' prying eyes. I took the box to the safest place I knew, the cave just up the coast that Great Aunt Kit had told us about a few summers ago. She had warned us that when the incoming tide rushed over the reef, the breaking waves would echo in the cave and we had to get out before the sea flooded in. There, in our secret world, we could be pirates and captains for a while. I wrapped the box in the tarpaulin that Da used to cover our bikes in the yard and I stowed it carefully in the darkest corner of the cave. There was a narrow crevice in the rocks that we could squeeze through and it was there, on a high rock shelf, that I left my treasure box.

We never opened the secret drawers. Jeff didn't bring his treasure box the following summer and searching for shells and stones didn't somehow seem the same without Great Aunt Kit to approve them. That was the summer we began going to the youth club disco every Friday night and the treasure boxes and the cave became a forgotten part of the past.

When we met I recognised him immediately even though the scrawny ragamuffin had grown into a lean fit form and I had to remind myself that he too would be nearly fifty-five. He ran three times a week, he told me, and he coached youngsters in high jump at a Leeds athletic club. He was recently divorced and had two daughters who were costing him the earth in university fees.

We raised our glasses to that and he asked me if I'd found my treasure box. When I told him where I had hidden it all those years ago, he almost dropped the pint that was halfway to his mouth. From an inside pocket he produced a ball of tissue and carefully unravelled it. Nestling within its folds was a single earring, a wide gold band, bristling with tiny diamonds, emeralds and pearls. He handed me a faded card and with difficulty I read: 'You know why pirates keep a single gold earring? It is their fortune and its value can grant them their wishes. Stay true to each other, my little pirates, and find your wishes in life.' It was simply signed Kit.

'Elizabethan,' Jeff said, ''ad it checked and valued. One's worth a pretty penny, but a pair....' he whistled.

We got a taxi to Seapoint. The tide was out and we clambered down the rocks, Jeff as agile as a cat. I could remember exactly where the cave was and once inside the smell of seaweed and damp brought me immediately back the day I had hidden the little wooden box.

'How did I ever fit through there!' I cried in dismay as I surveyed the narrow crevice in the rocks, the space I had crept through to hide the treasure box that I was sure was still sitting on the high rock shelf within the crevice. I watched in amazement as Jeff contorted his frame through the narrow gap and handed out a tarpaulin-covered package, sheathed in seaweed and smelling like something from a sewer. 'Done a bit o' pot 'oling in Dales,' he grinned. The echo of the incoming tide crept into the cave like a banshee's wail and it was a few minutes before we remembered what that sound heralded. We ran then, me clutching the precious box, clambering up onto the rocks behind Jeff just as the sea began to edge into our childhood playground.

My treasure, my box yielded the same prize. The beautiful gems seemed to draw life from sun as I held the earring gently in my hand and it seemed to me that someone spoke the words on my card aloud. Just beyond the rocks, where I knew it was too shallow for a boat, I saw a shadow forming and for a second I clearly saw a boat with red sails and on her deck a little border terrier ran up and down, barking joyously, before jumping to shore. The image melted before I could share it with Jeff.

'Did ye ever get the dog, Jeff?' I asked.

'Naw,' he said, 'wife didn't like 'em. Nearly got one the other week though, from a rescue place, but they wouldn't give her to me, said there weren't enough room for her in flat.' He stretched out on the rocks and grinned, ''appen I'll go back and fetch her soon!'

I turned the gold band over in my hand and lay back to share in his sunlight.

'Border terrier, was she?' I asked.

'Aye,' he said, stretching to the sun, 'name of Megan, bonny wee thing.'

Mr MacPhersen's Last Day

Joe O'Reilly

Macker fixed the man on the other side of the counter with a menacing glare. 'Ya gotta believe it, mate. Ya need protection.' Suddenly his enormous hand shot out and a quick shove sent the man sprawling against the shelves toppling batteries and bars of chocolate. 'See ya, Saturday.' He'd have no real trouble with this one. He'd pay. Sooner or later they all pay but it can take time. You just gotta know how to handle them. Take his next call for instance, Daly, the new one in Grogan's Hardware. He was different. He was going to be a problem. Macker knew it from the minute he set eyes on him. What is it about hardware? They're always the same, think they can do what they like. You can't talk to them. Stopping outside the shop for a minute he watched as two men worked to replace the broken window. He stepped inside.

'Had a bit of trouble, Mr Daly?' It was more a statement than a question. Daly stared at him frostily.

'Anything I can do?' He pursued.

Daly came around the counter menacingly. He was as big as Macker and in even better shape. 'You can get out of here while you're able,' he growled. Macker backed out quickly. 'Just trying to help, Mr Daly. If word gets around that you're a friend of mine you won't have this kind of trouble.'

It would take another broken window at least. The insurance company would refuse cover. Daly would be easier to talk to then.

23

Another couple of months and he'd be on the payroll like all the others. Still you had to respect people like Daly. They were very stupid but they had principles – and you have to respect that.

He swaggered down the street savouring the warmth of the strong summer sun. This was his turf. Here he was king. Three more calls and he'd be finished for the day. Then dinner with Bernie and the kids, later a few drinks with the boys, a game of cards maybe...

'Macker!' He jumped. As usual The Bodger had managed to get within a yard of him before making his presence known – an irritating habit that one of these days would get him a knife in the guts. 'Big Louis wants to see you.'

'Big Louis?' Despite the heat Macker felt something cold and damp begin to spread across his back. He shivered.

'Yeah. Four o'clock.' Bodger seemed to fade before his eyes like the ghost in an old film.

Glancing at his watch he lit a cigarette and took several deep pulls. Two hours. Time for another call. No, the calls could wait. Better concentrate on Louis and what he wanted. Slowly he headed towards the suburb where Louis lived. He'd walk. It'd give him time to think. A knot the size of a turnip had already formed in his stomach but he tried to ignore it. He despised himself for feeling so nervous. Nervous? Afraid, then? Hell, no. Scared shitless! A private meeting with Big Louis was not something to be just nervous about.Finding a doorway he glanced at his watch again and lit another cigarette. What did Louis want? There were rumours of a big shake-up, a new approach, an expansion of business. Maybe it was promotion, a bigger territory. Louis had said last year that he had big plans for him. This could be it.

His take was down, of course. It could be that. He shivered. But it wasn't his fault. Louis knew that. Times were hard. Everyone knew that. He rehearsed in his mind what he would say: 'Boss, I gotta have more turf. A couple of streets, maybe. A new area ... anything.'

With a final glance at his watch he left the shelter of the

doorway and sidled down the street to No. 43. A Mike Tyson lookalike opened the door and ran his hands expertly over him before allowing him into a room equipped with a large conference table. He perched himself on the edge of the chair he usually occupied for the quarterly meetings of territory bosses. It was very near the end of the table.

An eternity passed. He needed a smoke. There were no ashtrays. Big Louis didn't approve of smoking – claimed it was anti-social. He didn't approve of bad language, either, Macker reminded himself. Passing his hand across his forehead he was not surprised to find it damp. Sometimes – and this was one of them – he dreamed of going straight. He would take an ordinary job. Get up at eight in the morning, go off to work without a care, home again at six. Lots of people lived like that. Crime wasn't what it used to be, not like the old days, especially the protection game. Overcrowded. Full of amateurs that had to be kept in line.

The door flew open. Two giants strode into the room and stood behind him. He tried to stand up but a massive hand on his shoulder discouraged the courtesy. Big Louis followed briskly and took his place at the head of the table.

'Thank you for coming, Mr MacPhersen,' Louis smiled with his lips but his eyes were the eyes of a cobra poised for a strike. 'Your collection is down. You are having problems?'

'Nothing that I can't handle, boss. It … it's just a bad season.'

Louis' eyes bored into him. 'Sometimes people get tempted, Mr MacPhersen. Handling other people's money can be a great temptation.' Macker recoiled as if the cobra had struck. 'Oh, God, no, boss. There's nothing like that. I swear on my mother's grave. Every penny is there.'

'I'm relieved to hear it.' Louis seemed to relax but waited clearly expecting more. Macker tried to moisten his lips.

'It's the territory, boss. It's dyin'. I gotta have more turf.' Louis dropped his eyes to consult the papers that one of his stalwarts had placed before him.

'Mr MacPhersen. Your weekly returns make sad reading.

€4,632 three months ago. €4,107 last week. A fall of 11.3%. And you want more territory ...' There was a hint of disbelief in Louis' voice. Macker shifted uncomfortably. 'Two units closed down.'

'Ah, yes.' Big Louis scrutinised his papers. 'That was Grogan's Hardware and The Octopus. That would account for ...' Louis did a quick addition. '€201.' He raised his eyes and waited.

'I ... I've had to drop the take. From some of them only. They just can't make it. If I squeeze harder they're fuck – they'll fold.' Macker tried desperately to sound confident ... businesslike ... Louislike.

'Now, now, Mr MacPhersen, we're both a long time in this business. We both know you can never cut the cost of protection. It's bad for business. Word gets around. The clients think you're going soft and before you know it – puff!' Louis waved his hand. 'You're gone. I'm disappointed in you, Mr MacPhersen.'

Macker licked his lips. 'But they can't pay, boss. I've been through it all with them. It's true. They're skint. That's what happened Grogan. He just couldn't raise the cash.'

'Well, then he shouldn't be in business, Mr MacPhersen, now should he? Competition. Efficiency. Survival of the fittest. That's the very cornerstone on which the European Union is built.'

'Business hasn't been good for any of them lately.' Macker pursued. 'It's all them new shopping centres. And they have a lot of expenses.'

'We all have expenses...' Louis' gold rings flashed dismissively.

'They pay taxes, income tax, PAYE, VAT and what have you.'

'Someone has to pay these things.' Louis interrupted with a hint of impatience. 'How else could we afford the system of law and order that we enjoy. Never underestimate the value of that system, Mr MacPhersen. Without it we would have anarchy, vigilante groups, total chaos.'

'Grogan had a Revenue audit. That's what done for him.' Macker detected interest and hurried on. 'He was paying us out of the till. His gross profit rate was shit – very low,' he corrected himself quickly. 'They clapped a massive bill on him.'

Louis clucked sympathetically. 'Protection should be tax

deductible. It's a legitimate business expense. We'll have to do something about that.' He made a note and leaned back deep in thought. 'I wonder if we invoiced it from an offshore insurance company.' He made another note. His face lightened. 'I'll see if anything can be done, Mr MacPhersen. We have to do the best for our clients.'

'There's the ... the shopliftin' as well.' Macker knew he was treading on dangerous ground.

Big Louis smiled expansively. 'Ah, yes, the shoplifting, Ms Malone's department. She has been doing rather well lately since she recruited those two new hands.' He purred for a moment then became solemn again. 'We need Ms Malone. Without her these people wouldn't have to have security. Security is big business, Mr MacPhersen, ... gives employment... makes a very important contribution to the economy.'

It was an ill-kept secret that Big Louis owned the security firm that practically all of Macker's clients had been guided to. Macker pressed on.

'When they pay for security they don't want to pay for protection as well.'

Big Louis raised his hand. 'Two totally different things, Mr MacPhersen. Two totally different things, as we both know.' Yeah, Macker thought. You pay tax on the security firm but you don't pay tax on protection.

'But security is tax deductible.' Macker could hear the desperation in his own voice.

Louis smiled, not unkindly. 'Just so, just so. But I was hoping you would have a suggestion, Mr MacPhersen, something innovative,' he paused before finishing with just a trace of menace, 'something that would get your take back up to what it was last year.'

'I just need more turf, boss. One of those new shopping centres, maybe.' Louis shook his head sadly. 'Ah, out of the question. They're all gone. We have a waiting list. We get in at the building stage now. Saves on the educational programme when the units open for business. No, there's no more territory.'

Louis looked glum for a moment then brightened. 'I'm sure you'll think of something, Mr McPhersen..'

Macker racked his brains for something to change the direction of the discussion.

'The amateurs have started again. The Octopus was robbed at knife point a couple of weeks before it closed. Brinkley blamed us for not protecting him.' For the first time since they started Louis looked annoyed. 'Clients can be so unreasonable. They want too much. What do they expect from us? Twenty-four hour a day protection? From everything? From the professional we can protect them but from amateurs...' He waved his hand impatiently. 'Who did it?' He continued more calmly.

'A young 'un from the flats,' Macker volunteered a name.

'OK. I'll get Mr Johnson to talk to him.' Macker shuddered. Johnson was the only man he knew who actually enjoyed breaking legs.

Louis brought the interview to an end with a nod to his two assistants. 'I know you'll take on board what I've been saying, Mr MacPhersen. We need an improvement, a big improvement.'

For several minutes after Macker left Louis remained deep in thought. Sometimes he wished he was one of the boys again. Those were the days. Being at the top can be lonely. With a sigh he lifted the phone and dialled a number.

By the time Johnson arrived Louis was almost affable.

'Times are changing, Bill. Credit cards, hole-in-the-wall machines, computers ... even the way people think is changing. We've got to adapt or die.'

Johnson nodded agreement but without enthusiasm. Louis might have been discussing famine in Ethiopia.

'Take protection now. There's a dying business. Too many calls. Too much hassle. Revenue is down all over. It's just not cost effective anymore. We have to reorganise. I'm starting a programme of downsizing on the North side.'

A gleam of interest kindled in Johnson's eyes. His sudden attention was not lost on Louis.

'I'm amalgamating Areas 2 and 3. MacPhersen has to go. Has

been around too long. He's gone stale. I'm making him redundant. Give him the usual package.' Johnson acknowledged with a grunt and a sort of heel clicking turn. Louis checked his departure with an upheld hand. 'He was a good man in his day. I'd like it to be an accident, Bill. The other is' – he paused searching for the word he wanted. 'It's bad for morale.'

Forbidden Fruit

Michael P. McCormack

I had been feeling crippled the last couple of weeks or so. But today, I'm glad I've arrived at this place and at this time. It's exactly three o'clock on the last Thursday of September 2002. My destination is the Annesley Bridge, Fairview. The bridge itself spans the great Tolka River, which in turn flows out into the Irish Sea. What has me here today is the destruction of a minor landmark; to be a little more precise, it is a very old apple tree and it lies maybe three hundred feet on the north bank of the river, directly facing the corporation flat complex. The tree itself was the source of many folklore stories that had inhabited and haunted the children of the flats in times past. But today the tree is living on borrowed time.

I watch as the mechanical monster slowly makes its way towards the nightmares of my youth and, frequently now in my middle age, I feel my spirits lift. My thoughts began to drift back to the past. It was a past that was much more comprehensible than the present. After all, children these days are decked out in tracksuits and designer labels. Our labels bore the famous SVP, the special Saint Vinnie label for the under-privileged. Children now holiday in various parts of the globe. The furthest my generation ever went was Balbriggan, County Dublin, and the famous Sunshine House. These days, kids confine themselves to their rooms; play stations, videos and the like. In my day we were always out and about, scampering and scavenging.

My thoughts again return to my demon, the tree. It seems to have a sort of hold on me, maybe I should rephrase that, it has a hold on me, and it holds my soul and the souls of the orchard gang well within its bark. The once famous orchard gang consisted of me, Tony Pope, his cousin Robert Knowles and fat Marty Marks. Tony and myself were the climbers, Robbie, who was afraid of heights, would stay around the middle branches and Marty would work the bottom branches cleaning the tree quicker than the rest of us. That summer of '74 was truly a glorious year for us; we robbed every orchard from Drumcondra to Clontarf to East wall. Not only did it keep us active physically, it also kept our bowels permanently on the move. We were that famous we even had our own fan club, which wasn't bad for a group of twelve year olds. Marty was the entrepreneur of the group, who sold orchard locations for Dime bars, Calypso bars and Tayto crisps. A bar of Cadbury's gained you knowledge of the best orchards, especially if it was a bar of Whole Nut.

The only tree that hadn't been relieved of its fruit that year was the one facing the flats. And needless to say, the orchard gang spent many many nights planning the liberation of its fruit. Scavenging around the grounds of the Clonliffe College that summer we came across a battered old fibreglass boat tied up to the riverbank. Without haste the four of us liberated the boat. Marty being overweight nearly capsized us. So upon eviction from the boat by the three of us, it was easy to see he was openly disgusted at first. But I can still remember his eyes lighting up as he challenged us. 'If I reached the flats before youse do, I want a place on the boat. If I lose, I still get to keep the spoils from the tree' Marty chided.

In order to see him happy, we agreed. So the three of us using tree branches began to row like Vikings. Needless to say, Marty was sitting in the flats hours before we arrived. I never thought it would be so hard to row a boat. Again we reached the flats the tide was nearly out, forcing us to abandon the rowing. The river

being knee deep, Robbie and myself had to climb out of the boat
and pull it to shore. Tony was whimpering he couldn't swim.
Robbie and me were slagging him off; we both knew he didn't
want to get wet. We finally managed after a struggle to pull the
boat in under the Richmond Road Bridge.

Tony volunteered to fetch some rope so we could tie up the
boat. A little later he returned with Marty who found Robbie
and me soaking wet absolutely hilarious, so hilarious that his
laughter caused him to stumble and trip, sending him rolling off
the bank and into the water. Tony, the clever dick, was
determined that the same fate would not befall him and climbed
over the small wall and vanished without warning.

The next morning the rest of the orchard gang and me were
shifted to the Sunshine House for a week, along with ten other
boys from the flats. 'Ballor' as it was called to anybody that had
ever visited it, was a haven for boys. There was everything a boy
could think of doing. During the day there was football, treasure
hunts, collecting jackstones and winkles on the beach. In the
evening there were pantomimes and movies, along with musical
chairs. But every night the four of us would separate from the
rest of the boys. The boat and the tree was our nightly
discussion. We would call a skipper conference. We decided that
myself, Tony and Robbie, would cross the Tolka at high tide. The
rising tide would give us extra leverage leaving only about eight
feet of wall to climb. All the apples would be returned to the
newly crowned head skipper Marty. Since he was not crossing
the river, he was absolutely delighted with his newly acquired
title.

The Friday before we were due back from 'Ballor' we decided
to play on the monkey-puzzle; I slipped and broke my arm. To this
day I can't remember the pain, only the disappointment of going
home on my own. My arm got fixed up in Jervis Street and while
sitting in Casualty, it suddenly dawned on me that I wouldn't be
part of the crossing. I broke down crying. My mother thought to
her dying day that my broken arm had caused the tears.

When they returned from Ballor the next day at six o'clock in the evening I was waiting in the flats for them. Earlier that day I had ventured over to where the boat was docked under the bridge. On seeing it was still tied up, it took me nearly two hours to climb over the small wall that led back to the flats. It finally hit home then and there, that Marty would be making the crossing instead of me.

Sunday at three thirty on the warmest day of that year, the four of us sat watching the tide reach its peak. Earlier that morning we had dragged the boat into place and tied it off, directly facing our challenge. Four o'clock and full tide beckoned. A look of sadness crossed the faces of my friends, even Marty, when they fully understood that I would be remaining behind. I watched with envy as they climbed the railings, descended the wall and into the battered boat. Tears welled up in my eyes as they set sail.

The sailing didn't go unnoticed. One child called out to another and before they were half way across, there was a crowd of boys and girls cheering them on. Some of the older boys were sitting atop the railings and in danger of falling into the river. I, as well as the rest of the crowd held our collective breath as the three adventurers reached the wall on the other side of the river, a perfect landing. Directly over their heads hung the prize. Suddenly somebody on this side of the river began to scream 'Do it, do it'

My lungs and ears threatened to burst as my scream reached a crescendo. Tony and Robbie were climbing the wall, Marty was using his fingers clinging to a piece of rock holding the boat in its moorings. There was a tumultuous roar as the two boys had reached the top. I was clapping. The boys and girls around me were jumping with unbridled joy.

Then the day suddenly turned dark, the sun covered its face. I knew something was wrong. I yelled to them to return. My voice was lost along the river.I watched stunned as Robbie reached out to take the first apple and the wall crumbled. Tony and Robbie hit the water followed by a ton of bricks. More bricks landed on the boat sending Marty spiralling into the air.

He landed in the water but never surfaced. The scene still haunts my nightmares. Myself and the other children descended into a shocked silence. Then suddenly an unmerciful scream erupted from the flats. Parents were running towards children, who in turn were being dragged inside their doors. I couldn't move. Tony's mother was first on the scene; I remember her asking me what happened. 'They're all in the water' I cried.

Later that night I watched from the balcony as they retrieved the bodies of my friends. Tony and Robbie had drowned under the weight of the falling wall; Marty had been impaled on the frame of a bike that had been lying on the riverbed since long before I was born. Glancing towards the tree that night I swear its reflection gave off a sinister smile in the water.

My thoughts return to the present. Glancing towards the metal monster as it spluttered and stalled before the apple front tree, a voice in the back of my head is screaming 'For the orchard crew.'

Then the monster's engine dies. My heart sinks. Turning towards sky, I beg my god not to let this happen. The engine sparks into life again. I feel a sadistic urge run through me as the iron teeth of the monster grabs at the trunk of the demon tree. Suddenly I feel an excruciating pain in my spine. The tree knows why I'm here. I go weak at the knees, the ground trembles from the roots being violently torn from the earth. I won't be deterred. Raising my head again in time to see the monster rip at the tree. Witnessing this event makes me vomit into the river.

A man standing beside me asks am I okay? I mumble something affirmative through tearful eyes. Immense relief engulfs my body as the tree is finally tossed into the water. Revenge is mine even if my hand did not do the deed. Then something strange happens, or maybe my eyes are deceiving me. The tree begins to dance, the sky grows dark, it then suddenly explodes, lightning strikes from the heavens turning the tree into an inferno. I feel the pain of my youth slowly subside as I gingerly climb to my feet using the railing of the bridge for support. In disbelief, I watch what I can only call souls begin

rising from the blazing shrub. The last of these souls, and there
are three, make their way directly towards me. It's Tony, Robbie
and Marty, smiling. I watch their lips move, but there's no
sound. I can honestly say that they are saying
  'Aye aye skipper.'
Standing to my feet and reaching out to touch the apparition,
it becomes transparent and vanishes into thin air. I turn and
walk unsteadily from the bridge. A few minutes later, I find
myself walking as freely as a child. Gone are the crippling pains.
I smile as I watch my shadow dancing on the ground. I am
walking with a swagger.

The Day of the Hunter

Brian McCabe

Leaving the office for yet another crucial meeting, Ryan McArthur slipped on his Armani shades so that he could watch junior female staff eye him as he passed. He seemed to reach out to some with a limp absentminded hand that ended simply in a light brush over the desktops of those nearest the aisle, bestowing on each a waft of Gucci but no recognition.

Having cocktails and oysters at his favourite "Raw Bar" he moved to block out the not too subtle exposure of a deep cleavage at the next table so as to give all his attention to Dexter, his squash partner and leading bondholder for Murphy O'Brien. With no other distractions about, he only had to show the initial signals of leaving for Dexter to do what was necessary. Each time he veered away from delivering the goods, Ryan's attention would drift until his quarry tried to fasten him for the evening by yielding what he wanted. It was the same at parties. People crowded around him babbling. The less he said, and he never said very much, the more they babbled. But this was business ... serious business.

So DAX were going for a flotation rather than a bond ... splitting shares no less. Ryan would make another killing when the markets opened in the morning. Such nuggets were worthy of another hour of his company. Dexter deserved that and besides, he might need to pass along that particular road again.

Ryan's three guiding strategies were largely responsible for his meteoric success. He treated information as wealth, negotiated through silence and only went to bed with beautiful women at the time and place of his own choosing. If he had three strategies, he had only one principle – he was the hunter – never the prey.

The leather upholstery of his Mercedes Coupe and the hushed mantra of its supremely engineered motor soon soothed the thrill of this latest kill. However, his libido became energized as the car responded to the slightest touch of his handcrafted shoe. He contemplated his options for the evening. Yes, a redhead … he was in a redhead frame of mind. Pressing a speed dial on his hands-free mobile he called Liz.

Liz was such a good sport, great fun, an excellent conversationalist and a fantastic lay. And most importantly, she knew when it was time to come and when it was time to go. Ryan never spent the whole night with anyone other than himself.

Her sparkling voice was as accommodating as ever. She had a bottle of wine open, a good book and the evening down for a stay at home but she would be delighted to throw something on and join him for dinner at La Cog.

On the way, he stopped off at the Shelbourne barbershop for a hot face towel and head massage.

The evening was the success he expected. Liz was one of nature's true ladies who never brought a pain or woe to table or to bed. She exuded charm, grace and a delightful ready laugh at the one; at the other, she was a porn star who talked dirty and acted dirtier still. Like most of his regular girl friends, she had a wonderful sense of timing, leaving the apartment at an hour that allowed them a night's sleep so that they might be fit for the chase on the morrow.

When she was gone, he stood in front of the bathroom mirror, removed his dressing gown and ran his hands over his tanned and sculpted body, pausing to regret the "Hicky" she had left under his right nipple. What a pity women can't do that sort of thing without leaving a mark, he thought. Their mothers should teach them … he wouldn't dream of stressing her skin like that.

As with everything in his life, he went over the details of this latest, if not unexpected triumph. Small things could be learned and used to advantage on another occasion. It was the habit of a lifetime.

The food and wine at La Cog were excellent and the conversation light without being facile. As for bed, he didn't believe either of them had much more to learn there apart from the love bite. He considered it uncharacteristically clumsy of her to have dropped her handbag at the parting kiss. Stranger still that she should have patted him on the head in appreciation of his bending down to pick it up for her. It was the sort of thing that a mother or perhaps a teacher might do ... out of character in any event.

He removed his contact lenses, marveling at the advance they were over conventional glasses that changed the shape of one's face not to mention what they did to one's image. Being tall, he had to stoop down a little to comb his hair in the mirror. The product he was using of late seemed to have left a shine on the top of his cranium. Not very cool, he thought. Perhaps he had applied too much. Using a small hand towel, he tried to rub it away but no matter how hard or often he repeated the process, the shine persisted. New experiences often bring with them new emotions. Ryan wondered if this one was panic as he rummaged in the silver, antique snuffbox for his contacts. Twenty-twenty vision restored, the fact became undeniable – he had a bald spot.

There are an endless number of computations in the way humans present their hair and Ryan experimented with most all through the night. The stylised spiky look that had cost him a fortune was smothered in mousse and flattened across the offending pate until he looked like an emerging Arthur Scargill. Brushing forward with petroleum jelly made him resemble an extra from a Cecil B De Mille extravaganza. Sleeking from front to back metamorphosed him into a dead and dated Clarke Gable type but the bare patch still persisted.

He awoke next morning with an ache in the lumber region, a crick in the neck and the realisation that he had slept on a narrow stool, head resting on the vanity table. His first instinct was to check the mirror. It might all have been a dreadful nightmare. The light over the looking glass reflected on his bald patch like the moon over water.

He arrived at the office two hours late and moved through the typing pool, shades hiding his baggy eyes. No one watched him pass. Gaining his office, he closed the door a little too abruptly and immediately switched on his computer. The flotation was old news. Fortunes had been won and lost in the first hour of trading.

Calling his secretary, he cancelled all appointments – business, sporting and social.

In Search of a Uniform

Rosa Fox

I was looking for an office job – a real good one, mind, a quality administrative position. So I signed up with the local recruitment agency to see if I could find the job of my dreams. 'How fast can you type?' the recruitment consultant enquired. 'Touch-type or dicta? Are you familiar with Excel and Access?' Familiar with who…? The consultant looked doubtful but checked her computer and tapped a number into her phone. She mouthed at me as she waited for an answer. 'Any experience in a solicitors' office?' I love John Grisham and never miss an episode of Ally McBeal but I didn't think that would count.

'What I really want in a job,' as she continued to hold for someone on the other end, 'What I really REALLY want is a job with a uniform.' She paled a little as she listened and her colour continued to drain as I went on to explain that the nicest companies, those that respected the work of their employees, it seemed to me, were companies that took the trouble to provide staff with a uniform. And the great thing was, I continued, you didn't have to spend an hour deciding what to wear each morning. You just hopped into it and got going. She described me into the phone and said that that no, I had never used audio equipment, and yes, my typing speeds were a bit on the slow side. But she felt, she said, that I would do very well in the legal environment and would suit their requirements exactly. I was certainly willing, she smiled down the line, if not all that able. I might have made it sound more complimentary myself, but she was the consultant, not me.

'They're absolutely desperate for a typist, they're prepared to give you a chance.'

Everybody in the solicitors office seemed busy, I noted. And a bit stressed out, as far as I could see. But, more importantly, they all wore a well-cut uniform of skirt and jacket. It was in a shade of plum that would bring out the colour of my lips, I felt sure. I wondered how long I would have to be employed to get one.

'Is it always this busy or are or are you all just completely disorganised?' I hoped that making general conversation would get them to like me.

'It's always this – oh God where did I put the Thomson file? – sorry! busy. Sit there and slip on the headphones.' A secretary set me up in a letters file on my very own pc and explained that all I had to do was listen to the voice on the headset and type what was dictated. There was a pedal to stop and a pedal to go, and I only had to press such a button on the computer to create a new letter – really, it was easy and I didn't know what all the fuss was about. The hardest part was getting used to the strange phrases solicitors use. In reply to yours of the 12th inst hereinafter referred to as the correspondence. Now how many 'e's in hereinafter? It felt like typing in a different language. The solicitor, Francis, he of the disembodied voice, appeared in person every hour or so and took the pile of letters I had produced and gave me another tape to slot in the dicta machine. He would appear back within minutes with the letters all signed and ready for posting – it was clear he hadn't even read them through. Such trust. I felt a warm glow. The tapes kept coming and I kept typing. I'm good at this, I thought. I'm actually better than this. Maybe I should apply for a place in college and become a barrister. How hard could it be? Hour after hour, I seemed to absorb the stilted language of the law. That evening at home, my

mother asked me if I'd like chips or mash with my dinner.
'I will revert to you in early course,' I replied. She just gave
me mash.

By lunchtime on the second day, I felt I really belonged to
The Firm and decided to find out from some of the other typists
what you had to do to get a uniform. First I wanted to impress
them with my ability to manage the heavy workload.

'Does anyone else type letters for Francis, or is it just me?'
Just you, was the reply.

'Does he produce more tapes than the average solicitor or is
eight to ten tapes a day normal?' I think I was making headway
in the impressing stakes. They were prepared to chat anyway
and assured me that, although they were all kept going by the
other solicitors, no one filled as many dicta tapes in a day as
Francis. The office speculation was that he was building up
clients in order to go out on his own, open his own practice.
They told me he'd hired six typists in as many months and all
had retired with repetitive strain injury to their fingers and
wrists. 'Well' I said, 'all this typing doesn't bother me. I don't
mind a bit of hard work.' Then added, not wishing to appear too
brilliant in the face of others' mediocrity, 'But no one works as
hard as Julie. Which one of you is Julie?' Julie, they were
puzzled. Who on earth is Julie? There's no one working here
called Julie. 'Of course there is,' I insisted. 'I mention her in
every letter. She's the one who completes the documents, isn't
she.' I should know. Hadn't I listened to and typed a hundred –
a thousand times in my two days at the firm For your immediate
perusal, please find the enclosed documents Julie completed ...
Only as the incriminating words fell from my plum-coloured
lips, did I know that it was documents duly completed I should
have been typing. The astounded faces around me broke up in
mirth at the idiot in their midst and someone sneaked off to alert
Francis. I had a visit from him three minutes later. My services
would no longer be required. Not to worry, I told myself. The
Agency probably had another job. The uniform, though well
cut, wasn't a great shade of plum anyway.

A second agency consultant had replaced the pale one who had gone home sick with work-related stress. It seemed that Francis himself had been on the line to her and had demanded payment for time wasting and misrepresentation of staff's abilities.

'Be sure to sign up with other agencies too,' this second consultant advised. 'We mightn't always be able to match your particular skills set to a job on our books.' I didn't have a clue what a skills set was but I felt a touch of frost in her voice so didn't ask questions. 'We're sending you to Lockbind for a day. Receptionist on a busy switch. There's no typing involved. Have you any experience on a switch?' Did she mean a light switch…? 'The phone, the phone – an electronic switchboard? How good are your phone skills?' I latched on to 'phone skills'. At last, I had arrived. I can talk on the phone for Ireland and have been the main culprit in the escalation of my mother's phone bill for several years, or so she maintains. And now, for a whole day – and more than a day if I proved myself good at the job, I would have my own personal chat-line (in between business calls of course) all on Lockbind's bill. I beamed at the consultant. 'So you think you would be comfortable on a busy switchboard? That's great, because this is an important client. We wouldn't want to disappoint, would we?' We certainly wouldn't. 'Now… do you have any questions.'

'I don't suppose the staff wear a uniform. No, no, forget I even asked. Here I am in office heaven and I'm daring to ask if I'll be allocated wings. Forget about it.' Mentally noted to bring my little black book.

Well, I brought it, my little black book. But, far from making contact with all those long-lost friends, the little black book never even came out of my handbag. I tried to phone my mam at quarter past nine to tell her she could book that foreign holiday she'd always wanted because costly phone bills were a thing of the past. But as soon as I dialled the first digit the electronic switch lit up with three incoming calls. Lockbind Incorporated, please hold… Lockbind Incorporated, please hold... Lockbind Incorporated, please hold. I was doing quite well. Next I had to scan a list of about a thousand names to find the correct extension number and remember which caller wanted whom. Even when I dialled the correct code, no one ever seemed in a hurry to pick up and get the (by-now quite impatient) caller off my system. Weren't people supposed to be at their workstations? Weren't they being paid to be available for calls? The opposite, it seemed to me, was true. I even wondered if the building was deserted. I might have a word with the Managing Director before the day was out.

Use the tannoy to page people if you can't get them at their desks, I was instructed, and given a ten-second training course on how to do so. It made sense. It was a factory, for God's sake. Managers had to move about the place checking that people were doing their job properly. Otherwise, they wouldn't be doing their job properly. But even when I had called someone ten times over the tannoy, the caller often came back on the line to complain that he was still holding. And to my disappointment, the Managing Director of the company seemed to be the worst culprit. I persevered, but my temples began to pound. I've not been diagnosed with high blood pressure but I began to feel afflicted.

There was a button you pressed to switch the tannoy on. You spoke in your poshest voice Call for So-and-So on Line 29 or whatever. Then you pressed the button again to switch it off before you said anything else because the anything else would be heard on the tannoy as well. And it wasn't easy to remember the last part what with the whole switchboard lighting up like a demented Christmas tree with even more calls coming in. So when I put the tenth message through for the Managing Director, 'Call for Mr Guilboard on Line Five,' I couldn't help adding 'So pick it up quick, you incompetent freak and do some work for once in your life'. And yes, I had neglected the third and extremely important part of the drill. My shrill, piercing, slightly hysterical voice echoed at full volume through every office, the canteen, each cubicle of the ladies and gents toilets

extending even to the furthest reaches of the car park. Mr
Guilboard personally escorted me off the premises.I wanted to
ask him about the company's policy on uniforms. I was sure a
tailored trouser suit would make a difference to the average
employee's perception of self. Get them to the phones quicker…
get more business in… improve turnover… But he wasn't in the
mood for a chat.

In my next job, I finally got a uniform. Back at the agency, the
Director herself had replaced the one with the frost in her voice.

'I'm sending you to S&M Do-It-Yourself Superstore,' she
said.

'But that's a hardware store – you know I want office work.'

'Of course you do. It is office work. The job is in their
advertising department. Luckily, however, unlike most office
jobs, they do not require you to type. Neither do they need you
to answer the phone.' Not frosty… more withering, her tone.
'They need some help with a large mail shot. That help is you.'
Something told me I was slipping down the ladder career-wise,
but it wasn't time to get picky. 'Now, you've used a photocopier
and a shredder before, binders, laminators, that sort of thing,
haven't you?' It sounded more like a factory than the office of my
dreams. 'Well, anyway, someone will show you what to do, when
they give you your uniform.' Uniform? Give? She had spoken
the magic words.

'They're giving me a uniform?'

'That's right. And it's one of the strictest company rules that
everyone on the premises wears the uniform. So, yes. You'll be
allocated a uniform as soon as you arrive.'

I was to discover in that job that photocopiers mysteriously
jam when I am anywhere near. I broke the sculptured nail of my
ring finger in the binder and blistered the rest of that same
finger in the laminator. They asked me please to stay far away
from the shredder. Yes, I got my uniform at nine o'clock. It
wasn't a tailored trouser suit. It wasn't a suit at all. It consisted
of a black t-shirt with yellow horizontal stripes. And a bib to go
over the t-shirt. A black apron-bib with bright yellow trim. My

name was scrawled in red marker on a blue sticker and stapled to the front of the bib. It wasn't just me that was condemned to fashion purgatory. Every member of staff wore the same. Everybody from the financial controller at the top, down through floor managers, store managers, customer advisors to the guy who collected the trolleys in the car park. Actually, he got extra – a bright yellow and black striped rain-jacket as well.

I folded a thousand leaflets – they had a folding machine, but when it chewed up the first forty leaflets and spat out the pulp, they suggested I fold them by hand. All remaining nine false nails suffered a fate like the first. At last it was time for my mid-morning break.

'There's a canteen down the hall. Take fifteen minutes and not a second more. The leaflets need to be packed in envelopes before twelve thirty.' I couldn't face the canteen. I needed fresh air, to leave the stuffy office where those useless and terrifying machines had first refusal on the limited supply of oxygen. To get out front, however, you had to go through the store. That's where the uniform took on a life of its own. My black and yellow tea-shirt was like a customer magnet. A woman dragging a five-foot shrub marked SALE HALF PRICE ordered me to find her a trolley. A man clutching a wooden toilet seat demanded to know where the plastic ones were stacked. Two small girls pointed to a paint spillage seeping from under a pallet of kitchen tiles. I protested that I could not help. At the same time and far more effectively, my uniform proclaimed that indeed I could help and, in fact, was at the beck and call of every customer in the store. I pulled away with a polite word of refusal to each. Turned sharply right in an effort to shake my followers, but the woman with the shrub somehow got in front and blocked my way. More customers built up behind, attracted no doubt by the voice hissing 'I'm gonna complain to your manager.' I detoured down an aisle of bedroom furniture and got completely lost. There was no EXIT, just more and more customers with querying faces.

By the time I reached the safety of outdoors the fifteen-minute break was over. I kept walking. A customer pushed a trolley into my shins. 'Take this back, willya. It's blocking my car.' I limped on until I reached the bus stop. I got to keep the uniform, though I now think that uniforms are definitely over-rated and I certainly didn't want this one. But there was as much use returning it to the store as going back to the recruitment agency.

The Last of the Romantics

Marian Finlay

'You never married, dear!' Mother Stanislaus remarked kindly, kissing Sinead on both cheeks. 'Another unclaimed treasure!' and she moved on serenely to greet the other past pupils of our generation. 'Stupid old cow!' my companion muttered viciously, almost before the good sister was out of earshot, 'I suppose if I married the first man who asked me like others...' The unfinished sentence hung in the air, an intimation, that though she had had her chances, her spinster status still rankled. 'And when you see some of the wives,' she continued, surveying the chattering groups with distaste, 'you'd wonder what the men are like.' I said I thought all our contemporaries looked very smart, and tried to steer the conversation into less controversial channels.. 'Well, you haven't changed, anyhow.' she remarked, surveying me from head to toe. Secretly, I thought I had improved. That wine uniform had never been kind to ginger hair and freckles. In turn, I admired her outfit. 'I dress to please myself.' she said, obviously happy with the effect created by the sari-type dress topped by a colourful fringed shawl. On anybody else it could have looked ridiculous, but with her coal-black hair and olive skin it was dramatic.

We had not seen each other for years, and I was surprised when she attached herself to me and greeted me as a special old friend. Our parents came from the same West of Ireland county, and throughout their married lives in a South Dublin suburb had maintained a desultory friendship. We were classmates, and our mothers expected us to be friends, but we were never close. Even then, she had been flamboyant and bossy and despised the studious group to which I belonged. The Swots she called us, claiming that her group were the more artistic. In reality, the nuns did not consider them bright enough to study Latin, something I never had the courage to say to her, not even now, when she repeated the statement twenty-five years later. It had ceased to matter.

She had to leave early, she told me, implying some mysterious and exotic rendezvous, but she asked for my phone number, and impelled by curiosity about her life in the intervening years, I gave it. My own life had been predictably ordinary, Civil Service, early marriage to a colleague, two sons living abroad and a married daughter, one grandson, widowhood.

We arranged to meet. One meeting led to another. She had lived on the continent and had worked at a variety of non-specific jobs in art galleries, museums, that sort of thing, where she had to endure the begrudgery of fellow-workers, who filched her ideas. It was a cut-throat world out there she averred, and Ireland was going down the same road. Men, she told me, hated to see a successful woman. Here, I felt I must demur. After my husband's death several of his men-friends had rallied round and had helped me to untangle my problems. She had stared me straight in the eye as if compelling me to take a look at myself and said, 'But you're missing the point, you're no threat to anybody.' Duly chastened, I lapsed into silence. She continued with her monologue.

Sinead believed in plain speaking. She had retained her values, and always defended Monogamy, Fidelity and Romance, concepts that seemed to be as rare in Ireland as in the rest of the world. She made no apologies for being a Romantic but then, all the Laceys were Romantics and Dreamers. Like all Dreamers she had been naive. She had placed her trust in people who had not lived up to her expectations. There had been an Italian, Leonardo, but his mother had interfered. Italian mothers were like that. She sighed.

It was only one of many such disappointments. I stifled a yawn. It was past midnight.

Weekend after weekend she sat in my most comfortable chair, drank endless cups of coffee, prevented me from seeing my favourite tv programmes, and re-iterated that she preferred the company of men to that of women. Women, she said were so boring and their interests were so limited, the cost of groceries, their children or such trivia. She found she had nothing in common with them. Men were so much more interesting.

I knew it could not last, that one day I would lose patience with her assumptions of superiority and her disregard for time. Often, on the verge of an outburst I restrained myself by mentally counting my blessings. One, I started, but by then she was planning a trip to some remote beauty spot or historic venue, and before I had time to fabricate an excuse I found myself falling in with her plans. I knew I was losing control of my life. Some day soon, I resolved, I would make a stand. Some day soon, indeed, so what was I doing standing at a bus stop on the far side of the city, waiting for Sinead?

I am not a film fan, but somehow she had talked me into accompanying her to see The English Patient. Naturally, the cinema was in her neighbourhood, which meant taking two buses to reach the end of her avenue where we had arranged to meet at one forty-five. At the last moment my daughter had phoned to ask if I would babysit that evening. Breaking an appointment with Sinead was unthinkable, and doing so at such short notice would be tantamount to lese majeste. 'Impossible.' I said explaining the circumstances. 'But I'm desperate.' She wheedled. We compromised. After the film I would invite Sinead to tea at my place, and at eight o'clock my daughter would deliver her four-year-old son, bathed and ready for bed. He would stay overnight.

Sinead was late, as usual. I walked up and down, fuming and regretting I had not brought a paper. Twenty minutes later she drove up.

'Were you delayed?' I asked pointedly, to show I had noticed the absence of an apology. 'You're lucky I'm here at all, I was feeling so bad.' was the response. I got into the car.

'Don't bang the door!' she ordered. Too late. I did. The handle came away in my hand. 'Leave it!' she said through gritted teeth. I wondered when I should mention Jack.

The noise in the foyer was deafening. Because of the mid-term break every child in the neighbourhood had converged on the picture house.

'Children!' she sniffed. 'I hope they're not all going to The English Patient.'

'Hardly! I think that's for Adults only.'

'Well, with today's parents you can't be sure.' The afternoon did not look promising.

After the inevitable wrangle with the girl in the Box Office we got our tickets. Knowing the probable sequence of events I had stood aside, dissociating myself from my companion, who was announcing in a loud voice that she could never understand the stupidity of staff in those places. People were staring and I led the way quickly into the darkness longing for invisibility

We sat through the trailers of coming events. Sinead settled herself comfortably.

'I'm really looking forward to this,' she whispered, 'I believe it's marvellous.'

Her mood seemed to be improving. I tried hard to concentrate, in preparation for the post mortem that I knew would follow. The nurse's behaviour seemed strange. I wished I'd read the book. Because of some flaw in my mental make-up I always have difficulty in following the sequence of events on film. Sinead has a name for it. Stupidity.

'Wasn't it wonderful ?' she enthused when we emerged into the daylight.

'He took a long time to die.' I commented, guardedly.

'Will you ever forget that scene when she visited him in his room? Did you ever see anything so romantic?'

I remembered it well. The married heroine, attired in a diaphanous dress, had hardly got inside the door when she was pounced on by the hero and the garment was in flitters. It looked like consensual rape to me, if that is not a contradiction. Personally, I thought the efforts of the hero to repair the dress so that she could venture decently homewards was far more touching, but I contented myself with saying primly, 'Unbridled lust!' Sinead's eyes were shining; she was living the part.

'But wasn't it really erotic? Just imagine if two people were mad about each other!' 'Well!' I said practically, 'Adultery aside, if that happened in real life, you'd never have a stitch to wear'. She stared at me in disbelief mixed with pity, and said sadly, 'You've just confirmed what I've always suspected, married people have no idea of romance.'

The film seemed to have restored her good humour, and when I suggested tea at my place she agreed graciously. Even when I added casually that my grandson, Jack was spending the night with me she raised no objection. She did include a brief lecture on the foolishness of being at my daughter's beck and call. I should let my family go and make a life for myself. 'They won't thank you for it!' she concluded.

Jack arrived in a flurry of excitement, wearing his pyjamas, clutching his Teddy Bear and a video of The Lion King .'Just let him see it and then pack him off to bed. He'll be asleep in a minute.' my daughter assured me. 'Must dash!' and she was gone. Sinead ignored the child, embarking on a monologue on what her mother would have said and done under similar circumstances. 'Changed times!' I said.

The video over, Jack studied this strange lady who had not even acknowledged his existence.

'I want to go to bed now', he announced, yawning.

'Wait till the lady has finished speaking.' I said. He sat silently for a few minutes while Sinead continued. There was no way she was going to interrupt a sentence to oblige a small boy.

'Fuck!' he said very distinctly. She looked stunned.

'Ignore him!' I told her. 'he does not understand what he is saying. They pick up all those words when they start mixing with other children.' I could hear myself babbling.

'Fuck!' the child repeated, more loudly this time.

'Now Jack!', I said,'that's not a nice word. Who did you hear saying it?'

'Daddy.'

'Bed,' I said firmly, 'say good-night to the nice lady.'

'Good night, lady.' he said with an angelic smile. 'Why have you a moustache?'

I led him away.

When I returned Sinead had donned her coat. She had never been so insulted in her life, she told me, and I had not even checked him. 'He's only a child.' I said defensively. It was never too early to start training a child, she told me . What he needed was a good smack, and if she had her way that's what he'd get. I thought of the old saying that the children of old maids and bachelors were always well-reared but instead, I thought it more tactful to say, in what I considered a conciliatory tone, 'You never had any children so,' I got no further.

'I take grave exception to that remark.' she said angrily, flouncing out of the room and out of my life.

That was three months ago. I expect I should have phoned and apologised. Then, I think of the long Winter nights, the fire, the books, perhaps a special programme on TV, Jack's visits. Oh Joy! Oh Bliss! Who needs Romance?

Whispering Cobwebs

Ann Rhodes

She'd always like old things, she thought, taking the wilted flowers from the faded jug and tipping the now green-tinged water down the sink. Not like her brother, Noel, who'd always wanted to be outdoors. With the jug half-emptied, she paused, remembering. Climbing, swimming, camping up at the Hellfire Club longing to see the ghost. He'd have died if he ever saw it.

'Kate! Kate! I need the toilet again!' She sighed, hurriedly emptied the jug and hastened to her mother's aid. Sometimes she wasn't sure who, was more trouble, her mother or the kids, but after her second stroke she just couldn't live alone any more. 'Life would be easier if Alice and Tom didn't fight so much; if they were more like me and Noel…'

'They grow up soon enough,' her mother said when she was settled on the downstairs toilet and, not for the first time, Kate wondered if she had spoken aloud. Ten minutes later she was still thinking about her children, wondering how she could persuade Alice to wear a First Communion dress in May when her mother roared that she was finished. At that very moment the postman knocked on the door. The parcel would be Alice's new swimsuit, the carrot she planned to use for the wearing of the pretty, white dress, so the usually impatient postman was tended to first. Her mother was swearing loudly from her throne by the time the parcel was signed for and Kate was wishing she

had taken Paul's advice and opted for the old folks' home out on
the Blessington Road.

'Oh I know yis never really wanted me here…' her mother
shouted as Kate helped her back to her chair by the fire. She would
sulk now until the children came home from school, then she
would start an argument between them so that when Paul came
home from work, the atmosphere would be fraught with tension.

Kate retreated to the kitchen, opened the parcel and laid her
daughter's new swimsuit on the table. It was beautiful, colourfully
patterned and sleek. She shook a matching swimcap and bright
pink goggles from the parcel and smiled. Her own swimsuit at
that age had been one of her mother's, tucked and tacked to fit for
her visits to the Iveagh Baths. Alice would never queue for an
hour for admission to a pool crammed with screaming children or
catch the train in summertime to the stone-cold outdoor baths at
Blackrock. At 6am three mornings a week, Kate took her daughter
to Waterworld at Abbotstown where she very gracefully swam
countless laps of the near-empty pool under the vigilant eye of her
private coach. Kate's coach and inspiration, she remembered, had
been the hazy black and white television images of Mark Spitz at
the 1976 Olympics. Still smiling, she repacked the parcel and hid
it at the bottom of the linen basket.

She knew her love of water had saved her life last summer.
She had forbidden the children to play in the surf that pounded
the Spanish beach but, once they were safely in the pool, she had
not been able to resist the temptation of the deserted beach
herself. She never really forgot the power of the final wave that
caught her, the gathering roar as she was spun round and round
and the bank of water that rose higher above her with each roll
of the wave. She knew she would drown if she struggled against
the awesome force that gripped her so she acquiesced, giving
herself to the ocean until the wave flung her onto the still
deserted beach. An ashen-faced Paul held her until she could
breathe and they had clung together in silence while the sea's
fury echoed along the empty beach, churning the sand and
showing them how fragile their lives could be. She shivered in

remembrance, losing her smile, as she often did when the howl of that final wave momentarily filled her world.

She lifted a shiny hardback book from the kitchen table. 'A Life of Robert Emmet: A New Study.' She had bought it with the book tokens Paul and the kids had given her for Christmas. Tonight, after she had washed up and when the family were watching television, she would go upstairs and read in that rare quiet hour of her day. She sighed. It was a far cry from the life she had envisaged when she'd walked up the aisle in the white dress that had cost her a week's wages.

'And it'd been in the sale at Clery's.' she told the fridge. Perhaps it was all Robert Emmet's fault. She had been a junior wages clerk when the company's Christmas function had been a mediaeval banquet at the newly restored Tailors' Hall. She'd worn a chocolate brown maxi skirt and a wrap her mother had made from an old curtain and she remembered how grown up she had felt. While her colleagues got drunk on the frequently refilled jugs of mead, she was intoxicated by Emmet's words flung passionately from the gallery by an earnest young actor. When the party finished in the early hours of the morning, she'd slipped away from the drunken farewells and walked home alone through the dusty, empty streets. She'd stopped outside St Catherine's Church, where Emmet had spoken those words on the scaffold, and she'd said a prayer for his soul. For a fleeting breath on that cold December morning she felt as if she had disturbed the cobweb threads of the past. Although she did not know it, for Kate those timeless threads would never completely merge into the dust again, never really seal the past from her imagination. Sometimes, they drew her to them, whispering, touching her face like the damp threads on the ceiling of the ghost train, reminding her that there was an old, hidden world all around her, just waiting for her touch. Kate had met Paul by then and Paul's passion was football so her young Sunday afternoons were spent at Dalymount Park and not amongst the old stones of the past.

She heard Alice and Tom arguing as they pushed open the front door.

'I didn't have to dress up for my Communion!' Twelve-year old Tom hated bringing his young sister home from school but Kate had insisted she didn't walk home alone. 'You did so!' Alice was shouting, 'and you're just jealous because I am a much better swimmer than you…' Kate sighed. Her mother wouldn't have to try very hard to start an argument today.

By the time Paul arrived home from work Alice was upstairs having already reached the storming off stage, Tom was practising penalties against the newly painted garden wall and her mother was snoring loudly to the accompaniment of Sky News. Paul called her from the kitchen and she was a bit surprised to find an amicable Tom and Alice sitting on each arm of her now alert mother's chair.

'Since it's your birthday on Saturday, Kate,' Paul said, 'what say you and I go out to the pictures. Into town, I mean, to a posh cinema, and maybe have a bit of a walk around Temple Bar afterwards–make a bit of a change?' Oh she knew it was her birthday– 40 on Saturday and hating the idea of heading towards 50.

'Be ace, that, Ma!' Tom's swinging foot kicked his mother's chair but there was no cry of complaint.

'Yes,' she agreed, 'that would be ace!' The microwave sang for attention and, assuring them she looked forward to her outing on Saturday, Kate disappeared into the kitchen to finish cooking their tea.

Saturday was one of those bright April days that threatened Spring rain but sent instead a soft breeze that made the bluebells peal a silently joyous tune. Paul insisted that Kate enjoy all of her birthday Saturday. They walked in Marlay Park and had lunch at the Eden while her brother and his wife looked after her mother and the children. They would get a taxi into town for the cinema, Paul insisted, which really was a treat as they usually went to the early show at the Classic on the cheap Tuesday night tickets. After the cinema, they would stroll to Temple Bar, have a meal wherever she fancied and have a drink in one of the late bars the lads in work always talked about, then get a taxi home in the early morning hours if Kate wished. Kate did wish and as she held

Paul's hand in the taxi she felt seventeen again. She giggled. 'I'd never have afforded a taxi into town when I was seventeen!' she said and Paul grinned, thinking the glass of Chardonnay with lunch had gone to her head.

At his suggestion, the taxi left them at Stephen's Green. 'We'll do two parks in the one day,' he said and they both laughed out loud at their entwined memories of teenage summer Sundays with no football and no money to go anywhere else but Dublin's lovely parks. The Green was lazily busy as shoppers sprawled on the grass, tourists strolled and children played by the lake or within the crystal sprays that umbrellaed the fountains. They chatted as they strolled arm-in-arm and Kate did not notice that they walked, not to the Grafton Street gate as planned, but towards the Shelbourne Hotel. They had jay-walked safely across the road before Kate saw her children sitting on the hotel steps leaning against a small overnight bag. 'Happy Birthday, Ma,' they sang in unison and Kate was so surprised that she sat down beside them.

'Well,' said Paul, 'we'd best check in!' Her brother, Noel, came running down the street.

'Jaysus but ye can't park anywhere in this town these days! Happy Birthday, Katie!'

It had been Noel who had first come up with the idea, Paul explained. 'Find somewhere that's connected to all them fellas who died for Ireland,' he'd said, 'and book in for the night, just the two of yis. Our Katie'd love that–she was always reading dusty oul books about them when she was a kid and going to look at oul dark jails…'

'I couldn't find a hotel that Robert Emmet stayed in,' Paul explained when they were installed in their room, 'I don't think they had them then – but Diane, our receptionist at work, suggested here. She told me that it used to be the best address in Dublin and…' he paused and added sheepishly, 'and I remembered how we used to wonder what it'd be like to stay here.' He went to the window, 'I asked for a room with a view of the Green. Come and have a look.'

They stood close together at the window, looking down into the calmness that is Stephen's Green and Kate, for once, was not concerned with the past. While behind her Tom trampolined on the bed and Alice examined the contents of the bathroom, Kate basked quietly in the love of her family.

While Noel took the children home via MacDonalds, Kate and Paul got gently merry on the champagne that he had brought for them. They did not go to the cinema but instead strolled into town, along the quays and sat outside in the softly dropping dusk to eat and to raise another glass in celebration. Just before the dessert arrived, Paul pushed a leaflet across the table.

'I thought you might be interested in this–it's what Diane in work has just finished and she said Dublin City University was hard work but really worth it.'

'Dublin City University,' Kate read and her eye quickly scanned the list of history modules. 'Wow!' she whistled, 'there's one on Emmet!'

'She said she'd give you a hand at getting back to writing essays and things…' he said. He did not tell her how stressed Diane had been when each essay deadline fast approached; instead he told her how proud they were of her when she got her degree and how she had sobbed with quiet pleasure into the bouquet of newly blossomed lilies they had presented to her.

'It's my birthday present to you, Katie,' Paul said, 'if you want to do it, I'll pay your fees and make sure you have time to study–you know, with your Ma and the kids. I know you've always wanted to learn properly about history. What do you say? Do you fancy giving it a lash?'

Kate leaned back in her chair and felt the promise of early summer drift across the Liffey on the evening breeze. There was something else too, something that she alone heard, something that softly whispered like shifting cobwebs, something that vanquished the wave's momentary wail. She reached across the table and held Paul's hand and when she said that would be fantastic, she felt the cobwebs caress her face for, just then, the past and the present had fused for Kate at last.

Views of Swans

Paddy Ryan

He gazed at the crazy patterns being formed by the red wine careering across the white formica. These violent outbursts, that made him crush the goblet, were getting more frequent. They frightened him. And now, despite his angry confusion, he noticed the patterns were merging into a rough map of Europe. He fervently hoped it would continue all the way down to Gibraltar. Because John O'Connell badly wanted a glimpse, however make-believe, of those dusty streets and shaded alleys under the blistering Rock where he had scaled the higher peaks of happiness.

Feeling calmer, he rose and gathered the slivers, not caring if his hands were gashed. He hated the cheap, shoddy glassware. Not a thing in this room would have got a second glance when he was manager of soft furnishings and home wares. But, he thought, I must not forget why I furnished the place this way, or why I'm destined to see out my days in the damp, Irish midlands.

After discarding the splinters, he used a nailbrush to scrub the pinky stains from his hands. Lighting a cigarette, he looked in the mirror. The horn-rimmed spectacles gave a scholarly touch to the tanned face that was topped with grey, thinning hair. He smiled as the image rolled twenty-five years back to a handsome, boyish face under a shock of black curls. Durex

Johnny, they'd called him then in the York branch. While
everything about him was neat and well kept, John O' Connell
felt older than his fifty-three years. 'And this cheap poison
doesn't help, either,' he muttered, filling a fresh glass from the
bottle of Australian plonk.

Mopping the table, he saw that the wine had given up a little
way into Spain. 'Bloody typical,' he muttered, 'not even an
outline of Gib.' His last moments there were also red. The blood
of that Pablo and Alma making crazy patterns on his bed and the
crisp, cotton sheets with a design of daisies—one of the store's
best selling lines. How could she do it, especially with that Pablo
whom he'd sacked for laziness the previous week, he wondered
again. Lucky, he'd brought home the sample set of sharp carving
knives that had quickly changed the smiles on their faces to
surprised horror as he buried them deep in their hot flesh.

Hearing the tractor, he hurried over to the window. He
couldn't make out which of the Sullivan brothers was driving.
Twins in their mid forties and his nearest neighbours, they got
more alike by the day. Nosy buggers, he thought. They fed him
bits of local history in which they knew he was interested but
they could never resist attempting to probe his own past.
Although he was seven years here, they were still puzzled why a
stranger would buy this place. What they needed was a woman
like Alma who'd teach them that there was more to life than
fodder and cattle.

The smell of diesel lingered as John O' Connell walked the
short path to the gate. A dramatic orange sun was sinking behind
the black peaks of the distant hills. He thought of evenings in
Gibraltar and the red pokers of heat sweating him like a pig as
he hurried home to Alma. Often after they'd made love, he'd
hold her and whisper 'my Alma mater'. But she had as much
intention of being a mother as he had of renting his body to
Algerian sailors. They'd met soon after she'd arrived out from
Winchester to take over The Hairs and Graces Salon, near the
Almaeda Gardens. Six months later they were married.

Examining the roses cascading over the low wall, he noted

with satisfaction that the new spray was keeping the greenfly at bay. Cupping a flawless, peachy orb, he was reminded again of Alma. Dainty, blonde and topless on that beach near Estepona. And those long, white hands that would never give another body wave or another body shock as they slid under your waistband. Go away, bitch, he muttered, feeling his passion rise. What he wouldn't give now to stretch naked on crisp, cotton sheets, watching a starry Gibraltar night through that chink in the curtains. Contentment, like he'd always found in the English Cemetery—that cool, shady oasis that looked straight out of a Cotswold hamlet.

Going back to the door, John O'Connell looked around his living room where four prints of swans decorated the sickly, yellow walls. He'd bought this house for its views of the lake and swans. The serenity of graceful swans had always fascinated him and he admired how they got on with their own business, no interfering with others. Swans were a man's bird. They knew what they were. He wondered if he might have been a swan in a previous existence.

Door locked, he walked with long strides up the narrow road to the green ridge that became a curtain of red rhododendron every April. This evening the view of the lake was uninterrupted, except for the armies of midges suspended over it. As two swans glided out from behind an overhanging tree, he thought of the tablet in the village church, commemorating a young man from the castle and his sweetheart who had drowned in the lake, a long time ago. And he felt that his theories on re-incarnation might not be so far-fetched until a vision of the naked bodies of Alma and Pablo flashed across his brain.

John O' Connell turned to look up at the ivied shell of the castle almost hidden behind another thick laurel and stately, copper beeches. His own house had been the gate-lodge. He often wondered about the families who'd lived there. Opening and shutting gates through scented summers, winters of frosted parkland, waiting autumns and expectant springs of hardy bluebells and gentle primroses. People born to be alert for the first sound of distant hooves. He jumped as a woman asked:' Do you know anything about that castle? We spotted it from the main road.' It shocked him that he hadn't heard the car.

'Mid 1700s,' he replied quickly, 'torched in the troubles. Built by John Mansfield. The family later became Mansfield-Parkes when a son married an heiress named Parkes.'

'Really?' she said with a smile, 'And I suppose Jane Austen did research in it?'

'Of course,' he retorted, ' can't you see sense and sensibility all around? Not to mention the pride and prejudice.' Delighted with his own wit, he thought how starved he was for company, especially intelligent female company, appraising her dark hair, green eyes and low-cut blouse.

'Is there a pub near?' a male voice drawled from the passenger seat.

'The Mansfield Arms,' John O'Connell waved in the direction of the village.

'You're not a native,' she smiled, 'Would you care to join us for a beer?'

Ignoring all the instincts that had served him well for the last thirteen years, John O' Connell nodded acceptance – eager for stimulating conversation. The past is a foreign country was his stock reply when the locals tried to invade his privacy. But there were times he actually believed his own lies about a wife and child tragically killed in Kenya. The photograph of a mother and child, secreted in a second hand jacket from a Cape town huckster, embellished the lies.

'You've company, Mr. O'Connell,' Mrs. Reynolds, owner of the Arms, greeted them, her beady, brown eyes filing away every detail of the young couple. Seated in the alcove by the window, John O'Connell felt uneasy with the girl's stare. Sipping her lager, she murmured: 'I'm trying to recall where I've seen you.'

'Susan is Crime Correspondent with the Irish Daily,' her companion said, 'Maybe your paths have crossed?' John laughed but he could feel the wine doing somersaults in his stomach. Exposure, after thirteen careful years, should not happen this way, he thought, and recalled that the give-away for Nazi war criminals in Patagonia were their neat beds of blue lupins.

'Have you ever featured in the news?' she was asking. Surely the name change from John Leggett to that of an Irish missionary buried in Malawi, the plastic surgery in Tangier and the clean-shaven face, couldn't all be unsuccessful?

'Not that I know of,' he said, 'but we all have a doppelganger. I'm said to have a resemblance to Richard Gere.' John O'Connell chuckled and rose, asking: 'Same again?' Returning to the table, he told them of the local belief that a tunnel connected the castle to the Mansfield vault behind the church across the street.

'It's said to have been constructed during the '98 rebellion when Anglo-Irish families lived in great fear.'

'Tunnels were the peasant consolation of an escape route,' the young man said. 'Remember Carcassone, honey, and the fabled alchemists' tunnel of treasure?' When she did not reply, he went on: ' And Saint Michael's in Gibraltar with its legendary tunnel under the Straits, for the apes to carry their dead to Africa.'

Steady now, John, he warned himself, all that customer-service stuff was learning to keep your cool in trying situations.

'You've been to Gib?' he was surprised how casual he sounded.

'She did a feature on the IRA shootings,' the young man replied, ' and I went out for a few weeks. Apart from the Rock and the Molly Bloom associations, I didn't care for it.'

John O' Connell remembered the day the IRA people were shot. It was sale time and he was planning a trip to Manchester for next season's bedding. He was also planning to spring it as a birthday surprise for Alma. Terrorists had nothing to do with him. Not like when the border with Spain had opened up and business had boomed from the expats from the Costa del Sol. Among them was George Cramley, a London stockbroker, whose sound financial advice still allowed John O'Connell to live in modest comfort.

But an unwelcome spin-off from the IRA shootings had been the bomb scares at the store. Which was why he'd gone home that morning to find Alma and Pablo in his bed. Although the bomb was a hoax, it had exploded his world and the beginning of his six years on the run through the most desolate parts of Africa. I definitely do not wish to retrace that odyssey, he thought with a pang of horror as she asked:

'Were you in the Services in Gib?'

'Yes,' he lied, ' but it's best not mentioned here where Black and Tan atrocities are still recalled.'

She looked pleased. He could see her as Miss Marple in another twenty plus years. As raised voices from the bar debated the previous Sunday's hurling match, her companion glanced at his watch and said:

'Nearly 8 o'clock. We must be in Limerick before nine. Do you want a lift home, John?'

'No thanks," he smiled, nodding at his half-full glass, ' I can do with the exercise,' and he hoped his relief wasn't too obvious.

Watching them through the window, John O'Connell saw her animated gestures as she talked to her companion. He kept watching until their car disappeared beyond the petrol station and then tried to focus his thoughts on the plaque over the church door. Anything to divert the powerful urge to crush the beer glass into tiny pieces as a powerful image of two swans rising into the air crashed through his brain, their loudly flapping wings almost deafening him.

The Great White Moth

Alexis Guilbride

Jennifer knew it was there. It was always there, like an albino buffalo with wings, its feelers waving around its furred head, tapping silently on the glass, waiting for her. Her mother closed the curtains in her room before she went to bed now, and she was under strict instructions not to open them until morning. But she couldn't sleep for thinking of it. How could they expect her to sleep when she knew it was there?

Maybe, just maybe, it wasn't. Maybe it was gone, maybe it had given up. She had to find out. Shaking with fear she climbed out of bed and pulled back one side of the curtain, just a few tentative inches, then ran from the room, her hand clamped over her mouth to stifle the scream.

'What are we going to do?' Mrs. Hall asked, rhetorically, for she expected little in the way of a useful response from her husband.

'Move house?' he responded, predictably. Mrs. Hall raised her eyes to heaven.

'Can't you be serious for once?' she demanded. 'We have a real problem on our hands here. I think it might be sexual.' It was Mr. Hall's turn to roll his eyes heavenward.

'You think everything is sexual, ever since you did that evening class about Freud.'

'Look,' said Mrs Hall, 'She's fifteen, she's an adolescent. That's when girls start to develop these phobias, moths and snakes and things. It's all to do with fear of sex.'

'Well, you'd know more about that than me,' said Mr Hall, noisily turning the pages of the evening paper.

'And what's that supposed to mean?' said Mrs Hall, her voice rising menacingly.

'Just that you were a girl once, so you'd know more about teenage girls than I would,' responded Mr Hall, without looking up from his newspaper.

'Well, yes, I would.' Mrs Hall was reluctantly mollified. 'And I think she needs help, professional help. Something happened to her at Irish College to set this off. She was fine before she went.' Mrs Hall paused for a moment, looking bemused, then her features tightened and she said in a small voice: 'Maurice, you don't think...'

'Think what?' said her husband, putting down his paper and looking anxiously at his wife.

'That she was ...' Mrs Hall paused, 'that she was interfered with?'

Mr Hall pondered his wife's suggestion for a moment, then shook his head and retrieved the Evening Herald from its position on the floor beside his armchair.

'Not at all,' he said, 'don't be ridiculous. They watch the youngsters like hawks down there. Sure you have to give them written permission not to attend Mass on Sunday, for God's sake.'

'I don't mean one of the other students. She could have been molested by a teacher or, God forbid, a local priest.' With this remark Mrs Hall's concern finally communicated itself to her husband.

'You'd better talk to her,' he said, his habitually smooth brow creased with worry.

Mrs Hall's ingrained Catholic concept of sin, or wrongdoing, that which produces guilt, fear and shame in the wrongdoer, was focussed on sex, the central point around which all the vices revolve. Her acquaintance with Freud's theory of the self had merely served to confirm this attitude. Original sin and instinctual drives were explanatory concepts for the same reality.

Jennifer, on the other hand, was more inclined to an Eastern approach to ethics, though she was quite unaware of the source of her moral viewpoint. Nonetheless, she, along with so many of her peers, was far more in tune with the Karma Sutra and the sacredness of the cow than original sin and the fires of hell. And the massacre of the moths was bad karma, no doubt about it.

It had been Jennifer's fault, the massacre. It had been a warm, clammy night, an imminent thunderstorm rolling faintly in the distance. The bedroom, with its four bunk beds crammed into a space which left little room for the girls' belongings, was unbearably stuffy, so she had left the window open while they drank their nightly camomile tea in the kitchen. The Bean an Ti was a herbalist, and she plied them with the fragrant brew when they returned home after the ceilis, high as larks in the summer sky. It soothed and relaxed them, just as she said it would.

Jennifer and her friends loved their Bean an Ti. She was an ageing hippy and she wore long skirts that swept the floor as she walked, just like the Romany refugee women who were such an exotic presence on the streets of the capital, from whence the four school friends had travelled to this outcrop on the Western seaboard. Bean ui Flaitheartaigh, or Nora, as she insisted they call her, was a wise woman, a sort of white witch who had a remedy for everything that ailed them, and her entire house reeked of the potions she was forever brewing up on the range in her stone-flagged kitchen.

Their other friends from Dublin, who were scattered around the area in modern homes with more spacious bedrooms, envied them. They were the Buffy the Vampire Slayer generation, and, in the absence of a strong Catholic Church whose belief system had so profoundly influenced the lives of their parents, the spiritual side of their natures had reverted to an earlier cosmology, like cultivated plants returning to the wild. They all dabbled in Wicca, to a greater or lesser degree, and each girl attending the Colaiste innocently ill-wished the four of their number who had the great good fortune to find themselves living under Bean ui Fleathartaigh's roof, as each hoped to be the replacement for the one who might fall ill or victim to homesickness. To their disappointment, Jennifer and the others thrived under Nora's attentions and had retained their places for the three-week duration of their stay.

It was the last night, the last ceili, and the advancing storm hung heavy in the air. Even though the doors and windows were flung open, the hall was foetid and steamy as a tropical jungle. Emotions were running high in the face of impending separation, and the humidity did little to dampen adolescent passions. Lovers about to be parted by war or emigration in other times, other places, clung to each other at the foot of the gangplank with no more intensity than the Irish College students whom the morrow would scatter far and wide throughout the four provinces.

Jennifer longed to escape to the slightly cooler air outside, but it seemed as if the Soldiers' Song would never plod its way to the last bars. Eventually it climaxed in a thundering finale, and she and her beau of the past fortnight, Connor, a dark-haired youth from Tipperary, gripped each other's clammy hands and pushed their way through the crowd into the black velvet womb of the Connemara night.

The air was electric, partly because of the impending storm, partly due to the release of adolescent hormones into the atmosphere. As she and Connor walked the winding road back to their respective billets they paused frequently along the way to kiss and fondle each other, although they kept their desires in check because both understood the implications of teenage pregnancies. Several of Jennifer's school friends were already having sex with their boyfriends, and one of the more precocious had already had a baby. These were the same girls who had played Pass the Parcel and Musical Chairs at her birthday parties down the years, decked out in party frocks and white ankle socks. Jennifer had no wish to bring her own childhood to such a rapid end, so she controlled the urges which coursed through her body, unbidden, and delayed their gratification.

Although she had dawdled along the road with Connor,

Jennifer was the first to arrive back at the house. She could smell the camomile tea brewing in the kitchen and her mouth watered with anticipation, but she ran directly upstairs to the bedroom, switched on the light and opened the window. She flopped down on her bunk bed for a few minutes, expecting the cool night air to revive her, but the air coming through the window was like steam and gave her no relief. She was on her way back down to the kitchen when the other girls fell in the back door and they all collapsed, groaning, onto their customary chairs in the kitchen.

'I never thought I'd hear myself say this,' said Kathy, 'but I really wish it would rain, so that I could stand outside and get drenched.'

'It'll rain tonight, all right', said Nora, 'but you'd better not go outside when it does because there'll be lightning, and I don't fancy sending you home to your parents as a little piece of coal. Run the cold water tap over the veins in your wrists, that'll cool you down.' Pushing each other and giggling, they jostled each other for the best place at the tap and their attempts to splash the cooling liquid on their arms quickly degenerated into a water fight.

'Come on, girls, calm down. Sit down and drink your tea. The more you jump around the hotter you'll get.' Nora's tone was calm but firm, and they did as they were told.

They sat in the kitchen for at least an hour, most of which was spent comforting Aisling, the youngest of the group, who had become too attached to the boyfriend she had acquired on the second day, and was in tears at the prospect of parting from him.

It was late and the girls were at last beginning to feel sleepy. They wished Nora an affectionate oiche mhaith, then slowly trudged up the stairs to their bedroom. Jennifer, in the lead, pushed open the door and fell back with a scream, causing her friends to tumble several steps back down the narrow staircase.

'What?' they cried, 'what is it?' but Jennifer was speechless with horror. In trepidation the others cautiously peered through the open door and were confronted with a shocking sight. The room was swarming with moths. Round and round the central light they flew, crowds of them, large and small, black and brown and white, while a myriad others swooped and dived through the confined space, battering against the walls, beating their powdered wings like small demons escaped from the pit of hell into the sweet and pretty bedroom.

'Nora! Nora!' they screamed, but Bean Uí Flaitheartaigh had gone for a midnight stroll down to the beach, in search of a cool breeze off the sea, and they were alone in the house.

After a moment's hesitation they ran through the bedroom and grabbed their beach towels. They then began a frenzied attack on the moths. Using the towels they beat them in dozens to the floor where they spread the cloths over the stunned but fluttering creatures and stamped on them. Over and over they flailed and stamped until not a single winged insect remained in the air. All was silence except for the sound of their breathing as they stood in the centre of the room, flushed and panting from their exertions, triumphant. Suddenly, with a shattering crash, the room seemed to explode with light and the four girls screamed. The storm had broken.

The sea was calm the next morning, but the beach bore the scars of the night's elemental rage. The air outside had been washed clean by the heavy rain but inside the girls' room it was still stuffy and hot as the window was shut tight. Jennifer was the first to stir. Her head ached. Stumbling across the floor on her way to the bathroom her foot caught on a piece of cloth, and when she looked down and saw the lumpy beach towel, that which she had imagined to be a bad dream revealed itself to be a horrible reality. Gingerly she lifted the towel and glimpsed the mangled, crushed remains of clusters of moths. The scream that burst from her throat seemed to come from somewhere outside of her.

The girls woke up, and Aisling tried to console the sobbing Jennifer while the others fetched brooms and dustpans and cleaned up the mess with a great deal of squealing and groaning as they collected the corpses. When it was over the four of them sat on Jennifer's bed and hugged and comforted each other. Then, in a moment, they were all silent and transfixed as they watched a very large white moth slowly and painfully drag its body across the floorboards and out the bedroom door.

Cowering in the hallway outside her bedroom, Jennifer considered her options: she could prostrate herself with guilt before the moth and beat her breast with repentance (but how could she atone for the massacre and what if the moth was just a figment of her imagination?), or she could accept the moth, real or figment, as her punishment, and learn to live with it.

One aspect of her parents' religious beliefs that had always seemed particularly unnecessary suddenly made sense to her: the notion of original sin, the idea that we are born guilty, that it is in our nature as we journey through life to damage and destroy, despite our best intentions. We all carry the great white moth with us, we are all implicated in the sins of the world through our daily struggle to survive.

Jennifer's parents, for instance, killed mice in traps. Every so often, when she was eating a meal at the kitchen table, the trap under the sink would go off, with a snap and a squeal, and she would be appalled. It had never occurred to her that they were equally aghast at what they had to do. They had explained why they had to do it: safe from natural predators and left to breed unchecked, the mice would multiply at a dramatic rate and infest their home, driving the family out of it. It was part of the price you paid for a roof over your head. She had understood the reasoning, it was just that she had not credited her parents with emotions that in any way resembled her own. Now that she thought about it, she recalled that her mother always insisted that her father empty the mousetraps: 'If anything was ever man's work, it's that,' she wailed, and her father did his manly duty, white and shaking, close to vomiting. Her mother really would have been better able for it – she was less squeamish than her Dad. Jennifer was just beginning to discover what girls boys were.

Downstairs Mrs Hall studied the Golden Pages. 'Ah,' she said, 'this looks like just what we need: Terence Taylor, Freudian therapist, specialising in psychosexual phobias and related disorders.'

'Whatever you say,' said Mr Hall, 'you're the expert.'

Spider

Arthur Sheridan

It flows. Pushed on by the fluid. Rushing through my system. Like grains of sand. Through an hour glass. Numbing. Sands of time tickling. Causes itches then scratching them. I shift my position. The grains of silver tilt within me. Ecstasy reverberates from then flows back into them. The ceilings grey and flowing. Egg shelled paint curling. Crispy. Gaping at me then accepting me.

'Ann. Ann.' Ann. The name I hate. My name. Practical. Purely functional. No frills. No letters wasted. Dull. Then again, everybody hates their name. Don't they? 'Ann.' He calls in his old voice. In this house of old. Old house. Old people. Old smells. Dark old, sad old. Old and cranky. Too old to be a parent. Then again, he's not my parent. The spider swings and spindles. Dangling, swinging, jumping, frolicking. On liquid crystal gossamer. Climbing and swinging from the curling paint crisp, where he sleeps, to the light flex. Building a fine mesh. Happily swinging.

'Ann.' He cries for me to come. His weak croaky old voice. Why call me now? Now that I was content with my cloud mattress buzzing under my bum. An unhappy man. A miserable man. A man that always needed looking after, not a man for tact. Oh no.

'We're not you're real parents,' he said. My heart dropped

through my stomach and thumped my seat. Flossie made faces at
him to shut his mouth, but oh no. He had to tell. I was dazed. I
floated on a sick sea. Their voices distant like background noise.
Yet clear like speaking through a mesh filter. A thumping in my
chest. Pumping.

'Yiz are liars, liars,' I thought to myself. A cruel joke. A trick.
Fourteen is too old to be told. Too old.

Eleven kids. They couldn't look after them all, so they gave
you to us, 'Flossie explained. Kind Flossie. Flossie couldn't have
kids. He looked pained at her kindness. He always looked
pained. Like a wounded animal. Jealous of other's comfort.
Always ready to inflict pain himself. They'd given me away. Me.
Away. To who? To these people. Old people. Drunk old people.
Always time for another one. Never pass a pub. They couldn't
have known. My real parents couldn't have known. They
wouldn't have left me with these people. Not these people.
Playing outside the pub. Years of it. How many oranges and
packets of crisps can you eat anyway. I can smell the soul of pubs.
Brown pubs. Brown air. Brown stained hands. Brown smell,
Guinness, sweat and nicotine, Rising off everything. Floor.
Furniture. Bar. Walls. Clothes. People. People glad to see me.

'Ah she's a lovely girl. Sit on me knee. Oh she's getting very
tall.' Whiskey breath. Porter Breath. Red nose. Old hands.
Yellow wrinkled hands. Brown stained hands. Touching, feeling,
creeping, seeking. Escape to the toilet. Wet floor, damp air,
Dettol smell. Dark, grey, peeling curling. No refuge here. Into
the noise again. Faces through a smoke cloud. Yellow smiles. The
noise of laughter and spittle. Gaping mouths. Yellow teeth. The
stagger. The swaying. The slowing, of movement and time. The
time warp of drunk. The laughter so easily turning to anger.
Simmering. Waiting for an excuse to escape. A joke not laughed
at. A hero turned down. I grabbed my coat. Make my way to the
door away from molesting eyes. To the dull grey light outside.
My saviours in my pocket. Grey. Balding. Threadbare. But still
with plenty of bounce. Tennis ball were best. Even if old.

Where you going Bob. Down the lane Bob. For what Bob.

Grunts. Garbled anger down the lane. He sits there in the wet. Exposed flattened phallus. Yellow, wrinkled. Swinging his arm, cigarette stub in brown fingers. Aimed for his graying capped head. Sometimes content grunts. Sometimes angry. Mostly content in his lapping wee. Alcohol happiness. But it would wear off. Then someone would feel the brunt of his anger. Or maybe he would turn it inward on himself. Mind drifting with the movement of the balls. *For rhubarb.'* Safe in my escape but they would not work forever.

'Ann. Ann.' The buzzing fading. Leaving. Going, going, almost gone.

'Ann.' His voice weaker. Hoarser. Silver grains to sugar. Dissolving. Fluid slowing. Pump failing. Dangling spider retreats to curling paint. Better go to him. Maybe he'll know. He's always suspicious. He knows something. Probably checked his pockets, knows he's short. 'You spent it in the bookies,' I'll say. He was drunk. 'Do you not remember' ha ha.

Try to lift myself from the mattress. Comfortable. Body doesn't want to go. Why call me now. So little comfort now. Try to detach myself from this feeling of effort my body's going through. I turn on to auto pilot. My body is light. Movement is slow. Like dance. Ballet. Deliberate. I drift down the stairs. Graceful. Light. I am a floating feather. Getting closer. His voice clearer. The door ajar. That smell. Dirty smell. He looks up. Glad to see me. Smell of fear. Me his comforts. His strength. I can see it in his eyes. So clearly. I'm surprised.

'Are you alright?'

'Ann, Ann. Thank God.'

'I'll call an ambulance.'

'No. Don't go. Not yet. Wait.' He's so frightened. Weakened. Grey face. Small face. Strength now only in his eyes, silvering eyes. I kneel beside him. His hands grab mine. White wrinkled hands. Sweat dampened. Cold. He's so glad to see me. He needs me. He loves me. I'm his little girl. 'I have to tell you.'

And I love you too, Daddy.

'It wasn't me. I didn't want to. I told her not to. But she

wanted a child so much. It was only to be for a little while. But she couldn't let go.' I loosen my grip. His tightens. 'Every day she got more attached so she sent out feelers and you responded. And settled. When they settled in London they came back for you. But you wouldn't go. You screamed the house down. I told her it was wrong.'

He tells me about my parents. Where they live now. What good. He grips my hand tighter. Looking for acceptance. For forgiveness. And I hold his hand just looking at him. Not any more loosening or tightening in my grip. Listening as the whole sorry mess pours out. His body hardening but his soul never softer. Confessing. Looking for love. But still not giving. And I love you too Daddy. Love. Poxy love. Love is for poxers. Stuff love. And he reveals the whole sorry story. Word for sorry rotten word.

'I better get the ambulance now.'

'No. Don't go.' The silver in his eyes dulling.

'You'll be alright. I won't be a minute. I'll send Mary in while I'm phoning.' Turning towards the door. I hear him plead for the first time ever. 'I want you Ann. Don't go.' Ah you'll be alright.

I went next door to Mary's. She rushed in at the news. I stood dialing. The man at the other end seemed routine and unhurried asking which service. In another time warp. The time warp of calm.

Mary stands over the body.

'He was just going as I came in.' The fucker was telling the truth.

'The ambulance will be here in a minute.' The ambulance, the police, the coroner, the social worker. The questions. Still four years till eighteen. Put in care. I haven't the time for this. I have a quest. I remember the address he said. I empty his pockets for something to remember him by. The cash smiles back at me.

I feel the bumps and rhythms float through me chasing away my sleep. Only five hours to London. Dust and cigarette ash and cold. Not like the ads. Expressway me arse. The address he said printed in my brain. I drift in and out of sleep brought on by my loneliness. Faces sitting apart. All sad. All lonely. All the lonely.

Where do they all come from. My stomach is acid and empty.
Mouth dry. Throat sore. Exhaustion overcomes discomfort. I
drift. I dream. I see him on the floor. His eyes fish like.
Inanimate. His mouth gaping. No movement. But his soul
egging me on. And then Flossie comes to me. Hugging me.
Loving me. Warm feeling. Warm to warning. Trying to stop me.
Controlling me. Telling me to turn back. Doom and Gloom.
Flossie the bastard. And then there they are. My real parents.
Clean. Articulate. Younger than Flossie and him. Loving me.
Caring for me. Oozing goodness. I hear voices. Hard uncaring
voices. They don't match.

'You're here missy. Last stop. We have to clean the carriage.'
I wake. In shock. Stunned. Noise. Train station noise. I'm
shivering. Cold. My head hurts. I see a face. An old face.
Cigarette in mouth. Irritated. Impatient at my sluggishness. 'We
have to clean the carriages.' I rise. Dazed. Go into the noise.
Confused. People everywhere. The sun is well up. Must be
about eleven. Where do I go. Which way do I turn. Bumping.
Bustling. Must find a way out. A taxi. Find a taxi. He'll know the
way. He'll deliver me. Deliver us from evil.

The house is big. Old. Worn. Dumpy. Still.

'Hello I'm looking for …' He listened patiently, expectantly.

'You just missed them love. They've just left for the church.
You got the letter then. Which one are you?' I made the church.
And everything else. Sick dream. Sick world. My heart lowered
with the coffin. I kicked in some clay. Two days. I'd missed her
by two days. She was the last. He'd gone two years earlier. The
others were there. All ten. Back to the pub. Porter smell. Brown
air. The others didn't seem bothered much. Drinking.
Laughing. Telling stories. Telling lies. Terrible, terrible lies. I got
up and ran. Ran and ran and ran.

I look at the landlady. She looks at me. 'No suitcase.' I nod
trying to look away from the enquiring eyes. Suspicious eyes.
Suspicion turns to greed. But I don't care. I pay anyway. And
rush up the unlit stairs. Into the unlit room. Away from the eyes.
Away from the lies. Anywhere will do. Just soon. Quick. The

light brightens the emulsion over wallpaper. Old pattern. Old paint. Paint curling on moulding ceiling. Bulb hanging from bare flex. Miserable. The mix dissolves on the spoon. Soon. Quick. Lying bastards.

'Drunks. Both of them. Dried out regulars. Each of us taken into care. One by one.'

Scum. Mix in, air out. Shove in. Suck in. My stomach tingles at the thought. Soon. Rest. The pumping starts. The grains form and flow. I drift and pump and rush. The grains rush with the fluid. Vibrating, Oscillating, reverberating. Their essence flowing out beyond the veins, beyond me. Filling the room. This is stronger than I'm used to at home. My cloud lifts up. Rotating. Spinning. Spinning out of myself. Ever upwards. Up to heaven. Up to the ceiling. And I lie safe behind the curling paint. And dream of spindling.

Love Thy Neighbour

Donal Twomey

A man can choose his house, he can chose his partner, but he can't choose his neighbours. Someone might say that two out of three wasn't bad. Guard Peter Hegarty would not agree. He decided from the off that his neighbour Derek Byrne was a man to be avoided as one would a dose of the Pox or the plague. He took an instant aversion to the man. He knew the type. From then on he referred to him as yer man next door.

The Neighbour next door was low sized and overweight. Hegarty firmly believed that due to his size and shape he was, to use Hegarty's vernacular, a cantankerous little hoor. That man could cause a row in a Trappist monastery as easily as in a barrack of soldiers, Hegarty proclaimed to his wife whenever his name was mentioned.

Derek Byrne drove a company car. He always wore a suit and his waistcoats, like the seed catalogue, were a riot of colour. His wife on the other hand was a petite little handful with dyed blond hair and sin tight mini skirts.

Peter and Joan Hegarty bought number twelve Carrigdhu Avenue. For some strange reason Peter felt that they had made a dreadful mistake. Joan was quite happy, having no regrets in buying the house. It was convenient to the Church and schools where their pride and joy, young Tom would be starting school next year. The gardens were as the builder had left them, a wilderness of broken concrete blocks, baulks of wood and broken plastic piping. The jungle had to be cleared and transformed into a neatly manicured suburban garden. That was Peter Hegarty's remit. Having done that the rear garden awaited his pleasure.

He consoled himself by thinking that the hard work would restore him to near physical fitness. His body had grown soft and flabby from two years behind the wheel of the squad car in Dublin's inner city.

Yer man next door got his done in jig time, what ever his secret was, Peter had no intention of asking him. Being a true son of the soil he decided that he'd plant potatoes in the garden once he had it cleared. That way he'd clean the earth leaving fine tilth of friable soil for lawn laying. The crop of potatoes wouldn't go astray either

A welcome break as Joan arrived with a mug of tea. Their tete a tete was interrupted by the untimely arrival of Yer Man next door. The man was walking and looked completely out of character.

'No car to day?' Joan asked, being friendly

'Would you believe it?' he asked them 'The 'Big End's gone.'

Peter was tempted to ask him who took it and was it perhaps a case for C.I.D. He decided against it. More than likely he'd give him a dissertation on the idiosyncrasies of the internal combustion engine. Yer Man was still talking, bemoaning his fate, Grieving almost to distraction at the loss of business. The meeting in Galway had to be cancelled, he told them, at the same time wondering if they appreciated the gravity of the situation.

'I didn't know Galway was on this week,' Peter said wondering what in God's name he or his car had to do with the Galway races. Peter had set himself an area to complete before finishing the session. So far he was on course. Another hour now and he could call it a day. Yer Man next door reappeared in his garden. He was all set for a lengthy chin wag. Peter continued digging.

'How's it going?' Yer Man next door was anxious to know

'According to plan' Peter told him discouraging any further

pleasantries. Peter dug at the same pace, turning each forkful with an acquired skill, shaking the rich brown earth free of the offending weeds.

'Wouldn't it be easier to get in a rotovator?' Yer Man next door asked. Peter looked at him as if seeing him for the first time.

'What's that?'

'Wouldn't it be easier to rotovate it?'

'Probably, but not as effective.'

Yer Man next door got the message. Without further ado he sought the sanctuary of his sitting room and the evening paper. That fellow and his rotovator. That must be what he did, trust him for the easy way out. A week's digging wouldn't do him any harm, probably wouldn't last pissing time. Peter continued to dig venting his spleen on the debris that was his garden.

Every evening Tom ran to greet his father as he returned from work. He'd search the pockets of the tunic for the elusive bar of chocolate. Joan argued that that was bad practice and he shouldn't be doing it. It was giving the child a wrong sense of values.

'Ah sure he's only a childeen and soon enough the brave new world will teach him the difference between fact and fancy.'

Late that evening Peter was nodding in and out of sleep, the toil of the day had taken it's toll. His limbs were starting to ache. A hot bath and an early night would be the Doctor's recommendation, Peter decided. Joan was reading Anne Swan's latest romantic fiction. The Radio Eireann Light Orchestra was playing Beethoven's Symphony No. 9, Ode to Joy. The peace and tranquility settled on the room. Peter was loath to leave the softly charged atmosphere.

Suddenly all hell broke loose. The peace and tranquility was shattered. An unholy row erupted next door. The sounds of screaming and shouting could be heard, cups and saucers were ricocheting off floors and ceilings, children crying added to the unruly din.

'He's killing her.' Joan said

'She's his wife.' Peter said trying to make light of it.

'Don't you think you should do something?'

'Not until he kills her then we move in.'

'It's not funny you know, and it's happening a lot lately'

'Don't remind me. 'That fella'd cause a row in a Trappist Monastery,' Peter volunteered for the hundredth time.

'They had another row last night but you were asleep. I was going to wake you'

'I'm very glad you didn't.'

'My big worry is that the people across the road will think that it's you and I are fighting.'

'I'm bloody easy about the people across the road.'

And as suddenly as the ructions started they died the death. All became mysteriously silent once more.

Garda John Ryan was Peter Hegarty's partner. He came from County Tipperary, the hub of the horse racing industry. He knew the formbook better than he knew the Garda manual. But for all his knowledge of bloodstock he knew enough to bet only on information he received from informed sources. The information wasn't frequent but when it came it was worth waiting for. To day was the day. The long awaited information filtered through the grapevine. The venue was the Phoenix Park. John Ryan cracked the code. Jack the Vicar, a black gelding owner bred and trained was making an all out effort to pay a handsome dividend, enhance the status of the stable, and pay the rates and taxes for another year It was all happening today above in the Park. This was the tip John Ryan was waiting for. After today he'd be on first name terms with his bank manager. His wife would put him on a pedestal and he'd redeem the family silver from his uncle's around in Marlborough Street.

As he entered the canteen he saw Peter at his usual table. He was on his own.

'This is your lucky day. In a few hours from now you're going to be rich, rich beyond your wildest dreams.'

'Oh yeah, I'll believe that when I have it spent'

'Seriously, I just got the good word, the brother rang me'

'Is it worth backing?' Hegarty asked trying to rise him

'Worth backing!' John asked (he was damn nearly insulted).

'That good?'

'It's a question of placing the bet and picking up the winnings. Are you on?'

'I haven't much on me'

'Beg borrow or steal and that's an order'

'That good huh?'

Peter knew John well enough not to ask the name of this fleet footed Pegasus that was going to make them both rich and shameless. Two thirty in the afternoon they were enjoying the contagious and carefree atmosphere of a day in the country above in the Park. The going was good to firm. A light gentle breeze reminded the punter it was still the month of March, the month of many weathers.

'Am I right in thinking that number five is in with a chance?'

'That's the meal ticket. Keep it to yourself, the less said the soonest mended'

The first race was for three year olds and had a field of eight going to the post. John advised Peter never to back on three year olds. The horses themselves didn't even know the winner. The wind started to pickup and a sudden flash of lightening was followed by a peal of thunder that set the punters stampeding to the shelter of the stands. In the rush for shelter John and Peter ended up on opposite ends of a crowded stand. The downpour started. The strong wind blew in from the East and seemed to carry half the Celtic Sea in its wake. The rain continued in a steady torrent. It beat a steady unrelenting chatter on the roof of the stand. The thunder and lightening growled and sparkled through the downpour.

'It's far too heavy to last,' the optimist said. After what seemed an age the rain eased, and the storm blew itself out. The elements and the two previous races turned the course into a quagmire. The going which was firm to good, was now heavy,'

'Where the hell's Hegarty gone to? Better find him before he does something stupid.'

The bookies were laying odds of sevens on Jack the Vicar. O'Brien's horse was favourite at evens and Paddy Mullins's horse was quoted at twos. The rest of the field was seven to one bar. He walked up and down the line of bookmakers and Peter was nowhere to be seen. Jack the Vicar had gone to tens. Where the hell is he? Damn it man show yourself wherever you are.

'Ah there y'are I was wondering where you got to.'

'You didn't back him? Please tell me you didn't back him.'

'I Sure did' said Peter 'I got him at tens.'

'Oh good suffering.'

'What's wrong?' Peter asked turning a light shade of pale.

'I tried to stop you, I couldn't find you anywhere. That thunderstorm has torn the arse out of it. The going doesn't suit him. The bookies are laying him off at twelve's. Ginger Rodgers'd give you a hundred if you asked him. He's not being backed. How much did you … ?'

'It's like this' Peter said 'if he doesn't win you'll have to lend me my bus fare home.'

Young Tom waited and waited. His daddy was late he's never this late he's always home early, what could be keeping him? The child would have waited till the crack o' dawn if he was allowed. His mother had called him. It was past his bedtime. The evening was turning chilly.

'There he is' Tom shouted and ran to meet him.

Joan could barely see him. He was like the prodigal son returning. She was about to go inside when she heard the child crying. At first she thought he had fallen. Peter was trying hard to console him but it was to no avail. The child was wronged, there was no going against it.

'What's wrong, did he fall'?

'No he didn't fall. It's just that I forgot, I mean I didn't buy him his God dammed chocolate.'

'Well it's good enough for I told you, you shouldn't be doing it in the first place, but you wouldn't listen to me. You have no one to thank for it only yourself. How come you didn't buy it? You should have known this would happen.'

'I barely had my bus fare home.'

That wasn't a bit like Peter, Joan thought, he always had a pound in his wallet for the rainy day and a fiver inside the lining in the event of a storm. Joan applied the thumbscrews. Eventually he told her of his day at the races and all it entailed

To say that Joan had an aversion to all forms of gambling would be putting it mildly. Here's the man she promised to love honour and obey till parted by death and only death. That same man went out and handed over his hard earned and sorely needed money to a conman. 'God almighty she swore I can't believe it, you, a guardian of the peace, a man paid to protect the public from thieves, swindlers, rogues, and robbers.' She laid into him. 'A ten year old child wouldn't do what you did.' She put the dinner in front of him. She did not wish him bon appetit. Turning her attentions to the wounded one she gathered him up in her arms.

'Never mind love I'll buy you chocolate tomorrow, your stupid Daddy gave his money to the bookies.' She put the child to bed.

When she came back down stairs, there was an extremely awkward silence. Nobody was speaking to anyone. Silence was broken only by the clicking of the knife and fork on the dinner plate. The silence was short lived. The jazz dancing started next door. The shouting and screaming was loud enough to wake the dead. Kitchen delph was crashing off the walls and floors. There was no let up, if anything it was getting worse. A full porringer crashed out through kitchen window and rolled down the garden. The sound of glass splintering could be heard at the bus stop. Peter sat there as impassive as a judge. He chewed with relish every morsel of food. He was deaf to the world. A charge of dynamite could explode in the garden without his care or knowledge. He continued to enjoy his meal. Say what you like but credit where it's due, his wife knew the culinary art as good as any, and better than most. She might not like bookmakers or barmen but she could do a steak with all the trimmings as good as the head chef below in the Royal Oak. The unholy row next-door continued unabated. Poor Joan was the first to blink. She broke the silence. Pleading with him to save the woman from murder, it was his job to interfere. How would it look in the papers if their next-door neighbour had killed his wife? He would be classed as an accessory to murder.

Peter finished his meal, giving thanks to God, and drew himself up to his full six foot plus. Then as solemn as a judge, he quoted the act of parliament, section, sub section, chapter, and verse with all the necessary wherebys and the hereinafters. They clearly stated that no man can enter another mans house without an invitation or on the foot of a warrant issued by an eminent judge or a justice of the peace. 'But' he added,

'yes' said Joan, 'what is it ?'

'There's something you can do'

'Me,' said Joan. She couldn't believe her ears. What could she possibly do? A mere defenseless woman.

'You could go down on your two knees and give thanks to Almighty God that you married a fine easy going man the like of me, for all his faults and failings, unlike that unfortunate poor hoor next door.'

In spite of herself she smiled, she never could get the better of him. She put her arms around his neck.

'Its only money he whispered we'll get some more next week.'

'And what will we do in the mean time?'

'Ah we'll think of something.'

With the help o'God and two policemen, Joan thought to herself, as long as one of them is not Garda John Ryan.

'How about an early night?'

Granny Smith – The Apple of Few Eyes

Breda Nathan

'Cissie, is that awful woman in the bonnet really our grandmother?' Tommy whispered.

'She must be' I answered. 'Daddy is calling her Ma.' Poor Rosie started to cry again.

'Go across the street and get tuppence worth of bull's eyes, I'll make us a bit of laurel cake, it's her oul feet.' Uncle Hughie was the only person in the world who understood or saw any saving grace in Granny Smith. He was our saviour on that first night on Granny's floor.

It was late on a March evening in 1913 when we arrived at her cottage on the North Strand, from a very rural Dundrum. We were wearing our Sunday coats on a Wednesday, always a sign of serious happenings. My mother was three days dead. No one ever explained anything to us, we found out about Mammy on the tram in from Windy Arbour.

'You were glad to come back,' Grandmother greeted us, addressing my father tersely. I knew he wasn't glad, watching his shoulders slump. At ten years old, the eldest of four, with little understanding of mixed marriages or the savage stands taken in those days, I grew up that night. My father ignored the remarks and changed the subject. 'Jane is dead and there is talk of a lock-out in Kennedys. All the bakeries are involved now. I had nowhere to turn. I have to go to a meeting tonight'

87

His face was thin and drawn as he spoke. I wanted to scream out, but I couldn't frighten the others. I was hearing Daddy's voice like in a nightmare.

She pulled a red hot poker out of the fire and flung it at the door. It stuck and quivered for seconds. We froze. 'You walked out of this house and married a black protestant when I was widowed only seven weeks,' she was screaming now. Uncle Hughie retrieved the poker and placed it gently back in the hearth. 'You go on to the meeting. I'll keep an eye on them. She's havin' shockin trouble with her feet.'

We were glad to go down the street to Huttons, the dairy-cum-grocer-cum-newsagents in Richmond Cottages, for the bull's eyes, it was an escape. 'Country mugs' I watched in horror as a rough looking townie boy at the shop door pushed our Tommy into Rosie and they both fell to the floor. Baby Mena cried out in fear. Despair gripped my heart until May Kavanagh stepped out to help us. 'You leave them alone,' she shouted as she pushed the thug away. 'Their mother is dead.' News of our plight had obviously reached town before us. The newspaper headlines screamed of Union and worker's struggles and strife, they were not alone in this. 'You get your messages, go on, I'll mind them' She dried their tears with the sleeve of her coat, while the bull's eyes were counted and we told each other our life stories in minutes. It was the beginning of seventy seven years of friendship.

May told us she lived next door to Granny and she walked to the gate with us. 'Mammy and me are afraid of your granny,' she said, 'It's because my mammy has a gentleman friend, but since my daddy died, your Uncle Hughie always brings me home crumpets and laurel cake from the bakery. He's a great baker.' She was afraid to come in with us, but we promised to meet the next day. Somewhere in my heart I still hoped we would be returning to Dundrum and Rosie was of the same mind.

'Cissie, could you bring us home, if we found our way to the tram? she asked. 'Maybe Mammy would be back.'

'She can't come back' I answered. 'Daddy said she was dead.' Tommy started to cry again.

'Does he never let you down?' Mena was frantic looking.
'Who?'
'Holy God.'
'No.'
'Not even on your birthday or at Christmas?'
'No. Teacher says that no one ever really wants to come back from Heaven.'
'I don't believe her, Mammy would rather be with us. I hate God.' I wasn't too keen on him myself that night.

Back at the cottage, Uncle Hughie was busy baking his cake on the range, as we shared out the sweets and told our story. Grandmother was reading the paper with the aid of an oil lamp. She didn't appear to be listening, but suddenly leapt to her oul feet with the speed of a wild cat. 'I know who that was,' she shouted. 'Their breed, seed and generation was reared on hush money. They wouldn't be fit to clean the boots of my grandchildren. Let me tell you, when I was a little girl my shawl and bonnet was put on me and I was sent in a carriage across town to pay the bastards with a brown paper parcel of cash.'

No one answered or dared ask why such a clean living family as ours would be paying the hush money in the first place, but it was starting to become clear that even if Grandmother was difficult to love, she might be handy to have at your back and that boy never bothered us again. Uncle Hughie picked up a jug and his hard hat. 'I'll go down to Gills and get you a drop of porter, Ma. Keep your eye on the children with the fire.'

She took her bellows and blew the fire almost up the chimney, then placed the large, now crooked poker in the fire and we watched it redden. To our dismay, she picked up a pig's head and scorched the hairs off it before placing it in a pot for dinner. We decided in whispers that we would live on bulls eyes and laurel cake for life, if we had to stay here.

Later when my father returned, the news was worse.

'We're finished, Jim Larkin told us. The pickets are going on this week. I'll have to sign up for the British Army,' he told Uncle Hughie. 'I can't be without money for the children.'

Turning to me he added, 'I may have to go away for a while. Granny and Uncle Hughie will look after you. I will make sure there is enough money for anything you want.'

'Please don't leave us here with her,' I begged. 'I want to go home. I hate this place'

'You didn't lick that off the ground,' Grandmother interjected. 'Your mother will never be dead while you're alive. You'll soon lose your ascendancy ideas here. Children should be seen and not heard.' I hated her then, my father tried to comfort me.

'We can't go home yet. Everything will be alright soon. I'll tell Uncle Hughie to get you your favourite comic cuts and when the strikes end, we can be all together again.'

'You and your modern ideas, answer you better to explain to me how I am expected to cope.'

Within a week we were waving goodbye to him at the corner of North Circular Road. At thirty-five, he looked like a hunched old man with his back pack. 'Is Daddy going to find Mammy and bring her home to us?' Mena's voice was filled with hope. We didn't have the heart to disillusion her.

Uncle Hughie was true to his word and even though there were difficult days at the cottage he made sure we had a sweet and the 'Rainbow'. I made sure to keep out of trouble and as far away from under Granny Smith's oul feet as I could. We siblings bonded together in a fantasy world of peggy's legs, bulls eyes and laurel cake. We gloried in Rainbow's Mrs Bruin Bear the teacher, and her pupils: Willie Ostrich, Tiger Tim, Jacko Monkey, Jumbo Elephant, Joey Parrot, Fido Dog and Georgie Giraffe. I shopped for Gran's messages: butter, tea, sugar, candles, rashers, paper and milk, eleven pence halfpenny. We saved a halfpenny a day and Rosie and I enjoyed Schoolgirls Own on Saturdays.

The cottage was the nub of the extended family and every week mysterious aunts and cousins came to visit and give their opinion on whether Grandmother should, at her age, be saddled with us. In fairness to her, I did hear her saying once that no grandchild of hers would be reared in an institution. A sort of uneasy peace reigned for a while until Uncle Hughie and Uncle James were locked out.

'We will not be dependant on Larkin's bag,' Granny said. 'My James is still an apprentice and cannot legally be locked out. No union will stop my sons from earning their living when they are prepared to work. I will take them to the highest court in the land.' Poor Uncle Hughie had no say in the matter. He pleaded with her to hold off.

'But Ma, we'll never work in a bake house in the country again. We'll be blacklisted and considered scabs.'

'Over my dead body,' she answered. 'I'll sort them.'

Sort them she did and Uncle James had to wear protective gear passing the strikers every morning. It was either that or the flying poker when he got home. One night a mob gathered outside the cottage door and we trembled in our beds while she went out to deal with them. I never knew what she said, but they didn't come back. 'Your Father or meself will never be constant in a job again,' Uncle Hughie wailed, behind her back, 'she'll get us all hung. Our names are mud in the bakers' hall.'

She celebrated by taking a trip to Dollymount on the tram with her two drinking cronies, Fanny and Mrs Fletcher. We were delighted to get rid of her for the day, but when a thunderstorm threatened, Uncle Hughie got worried. 'Cissie, will you go around to Duggan's corner and meet her with a brolly,' he begged. 'She'll never make it home in that weather on her oul feet.' I wouldn't refuse him anything but I knew what they were like and didn't fancy the idea of getting them home. As well as Gran's trouble with her oul feet, Mrs Fletcher had a condition that made her give little runs forward and Fanny had to keep standing to get her breath back. It usually meant standing one up against the wall and running back for the other. May Kavanagh came with me.

It was seven o'clock when the tram pulled in. We saw the demented look on the conductor's face and hid in a doorway, as he struggled and pulled and pushed until he had them all on terra firma.

'Do you know son, it's thirty years since I was in Dollymount,' she said.

'Well I hope and trust in Jasus, it will be another thirty years before you go again, Mam,' he replied.

We got them home and Uncle Hughie had her porter mulled and ready, this meant the very versatile hot poker being plunged into the jug. She eventually retired to bed and we sat down around the oil lamp to drink our cocoa and read our comics, that's when the knock came to the door. It was a boy with a telegram. I handed it to Uncle Hughie. He stood frozen to the floor, unable to read it. Grandmother appeared at the bottom of the stairs.

'I had something over me all day,' she said. 'It's Tom. He's gone. God's curse on the King.' Slowly realisation dawned on me.

'Oh no, no, it's not Daddy. Oh please tell me it's not.' Mena, dozing in the armchair sat bolt upright.

'Is Daddy coming? Did he find Mammy?' Maybe he had, we could only hope he had found Mammy, but he would never be bringing her home. Uncle Hughie tried to put his arm around all of us.

'Help me into bed, Hughie. I think God has retired and handed over to the Divil. Imagine taking young parents from their children and leaving a cranky oul crock like me that no one wants.'

'We want you, Ma.' He turned to me ashen faced,

'Cissie, she has lost four sons to consumption and now Tom, who she really adored. He was the apple of her eye. It's no wonder she's half mad.' If this was the way she spoke to the apple of her eye and his children, I feared for those she disliked, but for the first time I felt something of sympathy for her.

'We do want you, Gran,' I sobbed.

'Take a shilling out of the jug and get five peggie's legs, thrupence worth of bulls eyes and a slab of laurel cake, we'll worry about the money next week,' she said. It was indeed a troubled night.

After the terrible news sunk in, we knew we had no choice but to adapt to life in Granny Smith's cottage. Through Uncle Hughie's eyes, we tried to understand how she had become such an apparent tyrant, but it was not easy. Uncle James was not so forgiving of her. 'She will be the cause of a revolution in the country yet,' he warned. Maybe we got used to her, I'm not sure, but soon her stand taking and protesting became part of our lives. We had to march for or against whatever she deemed to be the rights or wrongs of the week and no one else's views mattered.

It was Good Friday of Easter week in 1916 when she went down the town to post a few letters. She was missing for hours. There was talk of terrible trouble in the G.P.O. for years after, but we never let on to anyone she was out.

Full Colour Glossy

Brian McCabe

Flynn Johnson threw two of her cerise tablets towards the back of her throat, flushed them down with the remains of her Perrier and waited for that magazine feeling to return. She had had it … had it in spades until he asked about her school. And while she awaited the reappearance of cool, she beat herself up for having blown it so totally at such a critical moment and in so public a place.

The buyer from Saatchi and Saatchi was not only a handsome bugger but his suit and hairstyle were straight out of Cosmopolitan. She could feel the glare of every young woman in the restaurant. This man not only knew how to dress but how to handle snooty waitpersons.

'As you've inspired us with your ideas for promoting tropical investment properties, I'm sure you won't mind my rounding off the experience by ordering for us both.'

It was in the bag … what could she do but acquiesce.

'You'll love the "Lobster Armenia". It's a fusion of Caspian and Mediterranean cuisine mediated through a subtle antipodean influence.'

'Sounds exciting. Go for it.'

'There is only one wine to compliment it. The Liebfrau Hoff 69', he said to the sommelier with a snap of the wine list, and then turned on 50 megawatts of charm towards her.

'Showed your proposal to Jamie and Pricilla... I'd say it's a wrap... suggested we finalise things over lunch?'

She was so excited she forgot her rule about mixing business with pleasure – leave out the pleasure. And so they talked and talked. He seemed fascinated about her ideas for using a stylised moon reflecting on the sea as seen through a car window ... preferably a Ferrari or Lamborghini. He loved the way it softened the image of the blocks of concrete apartments climbing up the hill into the night sky. She was talking too much and knew it was the wine, too much wine even before he ordered a second bottle.

And still he hung on her every word until she mentioned one word on which the whole event then dangled – SCHOOL. As she sat in the wreckage of an amazing opportunity she realised it wasn't the word so much as the way he said it. 'Red Hill High! That's a... school?'

All the lies and pretence that were her life came rushing at her: the facials recommended by *Executive Woman*; the clothes that draped seductively off prepubescent models in *Today's Fashion*; the house that featured in *Living Today* that had her and her partner mortgaged up to their tits. And all of it had fallen to ashes at the mention of her school. In the texture of his voice, in his amused expression, she could see 'Nit Nurse', dresses from the 'Salvos', the liberties taken at seaside eating-places where hotel garden tables were used by her family to consume packed lunches and flasks of tea brought from home.

He had hit his mark and knew it. He called the waitperson with a limp hand raised over his ear in a kind of royal wave and ordered two large brandies. When they arrived, he placed one in front of her. 'You can have that sweetie if you say something interesting about your education.'

In a flash, she had him by the knot of his floral tie dragging him across the table until their noses were virtually touching. 'If you were as smart with your dick as you are with your fucking mouth you wouldn't have to doll yourself up like a Sicilian ponce, you Wop bastard.' She was about to shoot her fist straight into his self-satisfied mouth when she noticed that his Laura Ashley tie was dangling in the Armenian sauce. She couldn't stop the laughter that came in the loud, long guffaws of the excited inebriate. Letting him go, she fell back into her chair, hands up to her eyes to stop the tears that were ruining her mascara. She saw him throw a fistful of bank notes on the table before making for the door leaving a trail of saffron drips behind him.

Cool was returning bit-by-bit. She straightened her back, slipped on her shades and checked out the room. No one seemed to be paying attention. If they had noticed her making a scene, they seemed to have gotten over it or gotten over remarking upon it.

Well, there were lots of companies such as his who would be delighted with her ideas. It was his loss.

Interesting shape to that skirt she thought, looking at the young woman taking her seat. It would look fabulous with a lower cut to the top... show off her flat tummy. Where did I see it? Oh yes! In *Girls will be Girls*, she said, singling out the magazine from the many stacked upright in her capacious Gucci leather bag.

Autumn Embers

Garry Ahern

Molly hummed a tune as she drove along the narrow by-roads of South Kildare. Her old white Volkswagen Beetle was well known as 'the doctor's car'. The trees and bushes on either side were softening and fading by the day now through their Autumn shades and variations. The clear sky was still well-lit by the late afternoon sun which hung low in the sky away beyond the Hill of Allen.

'We won't feel it to Halloween, now,' she thought, conscious of the oncoming winter and the wave of flu and respiratory ailments it brought with it. Anyway, she wouldn't have such problems too much longer, she reflected. She had already eased herself out of night and weekend calls. She no longer looked forward to the prospect of retirement as enthusiastically as she had when Arthur was alive. All the plans for leisure and for further travel together had become redundant when he died suddenly four years ago. Very much on her own now for the first time in her life, and nearing sixty, she had not found widowhood easy to come to terms with. Her two sons now both lived abroad. Loneliness and a yearning for companionship were no strangers to her, particularly at the end of a hard day.

Her social life now mainly consisted of evenings at the bridge club and her attendance at medical seminars, if the latter could be described as social events. Her life had been hollowed out, she thought, leaving a shell of sometimes frenetic daily activity which contrasted with the often aching emptiness of long nights and weekends. 'Here, enough of that!' she checked herself, 'mustn't fall into self-pity and melancholia.'

She continued to enjoy her work and she was held in high regard by the people of the area. This was as much due to her own sympathetic bedside manner and outgoing personality as it was to her late father who had for over forty years been the only doctor in the district. 'Dr Michael' had become something of a legend locally, not least for his role in treating wounded activists during the War of Independence.

When he retired twenty years before it had seemed only fitting that his daughter – 'the young Dr Daly' – should return to the area and take up where he had left off. In time, as she got to know her practice and the people of the villages and countryside got to know her, she became simply 'Doctor Molly'. She felt she really came alive when out meeting the people, young and old, on her rounds. This was especially so when, like today, it took her down the less-trodden by-ways. She began to name some of the townlands through which she would pass before the day was out – Kildangan, Rossmore, Ballintubbert, Luggacurran. There's poetry in there somewhere, it occurred to her – Arthur would have made something of that-he had composed several poems to her.

She consulted her notes and saw that her next call was to a farmhouse where two no-longer-young bachelors lived. Johnny and Petey Horan rarely called out the doctor. They were reputed to seldom travel more than twenty or thirty miles from home but it was said was that they both had travelled to Dublin ten years before to see President Kennedy drive through the city.

She shuffled her indexed cards.

Horan, Petey, aged sixty, the taller and more talkative one. He was the owner of the home place – sixty acres of Land Commission farm obtained by old Mike Horan when the Garbin demesne was broken up in the nineteen-forties. Mike, a former coachman on the estate, had progressed to land-owner and resident of the splendid and spacious cut-stone gate-lodge.

She had got to know the brothers reasonably well some years ago when attending old Mike during his protracted final illness. Subsequently, Petey had been badly gored by a bull. He had, under her care, made a full recovery from several broken ribs.

Johnny, aged fifty eight, was the quieter one, shorter and stouter than his brother. He owned the out-farm of seventy acres two miles away which had been left him by an aunt, along with a fine, but semi-derelict, two-storey limestone house. There was no record of a previous illness. She saw that the noted phone message merely said "body pains".

Both were avid readers, she recalled, supplementing borrowings from the branch library with purchases of job-lots of books at local house auctions. As a result they each had a well-informed interest in, and a curiosity about, the wider world. Petey enjoyed company and had engaged in good-natured banter with her during her visits. He was always very keen to hear of her holidays abroad and was prone to ask perceptive questions about the holiday venue, the natives of that country, their way of life and how it differed from his own. He was known as a fine dancer, with a gracious manner about him, and had, seemingly, had many admirers in the past but had never married. A pity, she thought, what a waste!

She turned into the avenue. One of the results of the carving-up of the old estate had been that the gate-house now stood at the innermost end of the avenue instead of standing guard at the outer approach to the long vanished 'great house'. Mature ash, oak, chestnut, elm and lime trees formed a dark colonnade on either side, meeting high-up, excluding the fading sunlight. As she stepped out of the car she was immediately aware of the distinctive and evocative Autumn smell of burning foliage. A plume of smoke drew her eye to a corner of the lawn where the embers of a fire smouldered. Petey emerged from behind the hedge, a four-prong fork in his hand.

'Hello Dr Molly, I'll be with you right away – I'm just doing a bit of clearing up around the garden – Autumn cleaning, you might call it. I suppose there's a season for everything – including burning!'

'Well, Petey, how are you keeping?' she asked, as they shook hands.

'Ah sure there's no fear of me' Petey replied, appraising her trim figure, 'we never died a winter yet, anyway. You're looking well, Dr Molly, if I may say so, its younger you're getting – I suppose you're only back from some exotic foreign holiday?'

'Well, no, actually,' she replied, secretly conscious of his appraisal, but not displeased. 'I haven't been since – for some time now,' she trailed off as they stepped into the hallway.

'Sorry, I wasn't thinking' he said quickly. He drew her attention to the state of a barometer hanging in the hall. 'High pressure on the way, it seems we'll be getting frost tonight,' he noted, tapping the glass with his forefinger.

'So, what's up with Johnny, then?'

'He's not so good, he's not grubbing much at all and he's complaining of the cold – but I wouldn't mind that–this can be a cold house. What bothers me more is he hasn't come out of the bed the past three days. He never took to the bed before.'

They passed through the parlour. Rosettes of varied colours hung on one wall, on which a framed picture of De Valera was the centrepiece. The sideboard held numerous trophies, which, along with the rosettes signified past successes in shows, gymkhanas, clay-pigeon shoots, and the like. Making her way upstairs she observed that the house was clean enough, just a bit musty and cold. The bedroom was almost in darkness. She switched on the light to reveal a double bed, with lockers on each side piled high with books. Johnny's face peeped out from under a heavy quilt. 'Hello, Dr Molly', he said, his hands pulling the quilt a little closer.

She established that he had no appetite and that he had a dull pain in an area indicated by him vaguely, and self-consciously, as being somewhere between his chin and his knees. In an attempt to put him at his ease she asked him how things were going with the farming. His eyes lit up, looking at her as he spoke.

'Oh, not so bad,' he answered 'we had a good harvest – prices are going up with this Common Market now. We'll be getting ready for the beet shortly. I think we'll be taking more conacre next year – if only this curse-of-God bloody pain would ease off – saving your presence, Doctor!' his eyes turned down onto the quilt again.

She explained that her routine examination would require, at a minimum, turning back the bedclothes. He gave no indication that he understood but smiled benignly at her, as if he felt that whatever she was proposing was fine but really had nothing to do with him. She gently turned back the quilt, then the woollen blanket and then the sheet. Johnny lay revealed, resplendent from neck to ankle in a heavy black bull's-wool coachman's coat. Twenty-six brass buttons ran in an undulating line the length of this spectacular hand-me-down, like one of those illuminated illustrations she had seen indicating stations on the Paris metro, she thought.

Training and experience helped her to restrain an urge to giggle. She said she needed to check his breathing and also his abdominal area to find out exactly what was the matter. Johnny smiled a beatific smile and said nothing. She made some small talk and began to undo the buttons about his midriff. A hand came up and deftly re-buttoned them. She undid five more buttons. Johnny smiled his smile and his right hand immediately redid them. The procedure was repeated twice more. On the fifth attempt she left her own hand over two undone buttons. He re-buttoned the other three. She undid five more.

'Two steps forward and one step back – oh Johnny Horan, you're great crack' she improvised, to lighten things up a little. Johnny smiled his smile and said nothing. She undid five more buttons.

After an hour of this he had conceded defeat and the coat lay unbuttoned from neck to knees. She could now proceed with her examination. He flinched as the cold stethoscope defeated his outer defences and even his pyjama top and met his bared chest. His smile faded a little. 'Breathing's fine, Johnny,' she said, having heard enough, without attempting to have him turn over as she normally would. She then proceeded to his abdominal area. Johnny's hands clenched, gripping the lapels of the coachman's coat tightly. It didn't take very long to find the root of the problem.

'It's no wonder you have a pain, Johnny,' she said, 'you have a swollen appendix – nothing to worry about, we've got it in time – we'll have you into the county hospital straight away and you'll be right as rain in no time at all'.

His eyes opened wide, his fingers extra busy re-doing the buttons.

'Hospital, Doctor?' he asked, his eyes fixed on hers, seeking deliverance from this threat of further indignities and God-knows what else. 'Yes', she said, 'the sooner the better – you'll be a new man before you know where you are.'

Four days after the operation Johnny was sitting out in the hospital solarium, wrapped in a handsome new woollen dressing-gown, chatting to three other patients, when Dr Molly called by. She recalled with amusement his apparel when she had last visited him.

'Well, Johnny, how are things now,' she asked, sitting down beside him, 'how do you like it here?'

'Hello Dr Molly – its good of you to call in,' he answered brightly 'I'm fine now that that ould appendix is gone – this is a lovely place, lovely nurses, lovely food but I'm not allowed too much of that yet'. He introduced her: 'This is my doctor – Dr Mol – Dr Daly – she's our local doctor and she got me in here for the operation.'

'I hope you're behaving well with all these nurses, Johnny,' she said, smiling at him. Johnny said nothing.

'Oh he's a big hit with the nurses here,' the man beside him interjected, 'they're looking out for a big farmer with a short cough and a long purse, I think. But his favourite is Nurse O'Donnell – she looks after him really well'.

Johnny blushed and appeared flustered. He said nothing.

Later, she encountered Nurse O'Donnell. Tall, fair, fifty-ish, no sign of a wedding ring – well anything is possible she mused to herself. It wouldn't be the first time a patient fell for his nurse, she thought, but she was doubtful if the seemingly impossible would be achieved in Johnny's case.

'How is Johnny Horan progressing?' she asked.

'He's doing very well – he should be discharged by the end of the week, I expect.' Nurse O Donnell replied. 'He's such a sweet man and a model patient – does everything he's supposed to'.

Three months later it arrived–an invitation to the wedding of Josephine O' Donnell and John Horan, and to the reception afterwards in the Castle Hotel, Athy. 'I don't mind going along for Johnny's big day – we'll be dead long enough,' she thought.

Since the word of the romance had got out she had heard much gossip and comment on Johnny's unexpected romance. Some of it was well-meant but much of it was catty and some of it ribald. This annoyed her but she made no comment herself. What if he had been manoeuvred into all this, she thought, maybe he'll be very happy with this Nurse O' Donnell and live to be ninety, now that his appendix has been sorted out. She wondered, however, how Petey would cope on his own. It wasn't as if the out-farm house which had been renovated for the soon-to-be-weds was exactly next door to Johnny's. She could understand how Petey might feel all alone in his later years in an empty house – she knew all about that.

The wedding was, to her surprise, quite a splash with over one hundred and fifty guests. She hadn't really expected to but she found herself enjoying the occasion. The meal had been excellent and the fine group seemed to be conversant with at least some of her generation's musical preferences. The wine was going down well – she seldom indulged since Arthur died. Having attended to his duties as best man, Petey approached her.

'Could I have the pleasure of the next dance, Dr Molly,' extending his hand to her.

'Certainly,' she replied, adding with a smile, 'its Molly – I'm off duty tonight, you know!'

'Right so, Molly,' he replied.

They took off into an oldtime waltz. In the course of the evening they had four more dances together. She hadn't been held and danced like this in years, she thought. Petey really was a fine cut of a man on the dance floor, his formal wedding suit a far cry from his farming rig-outs. What were those lines from

Grey's elegy that had been drummed into them in boarding school? 'Full many a flower is born to blush unseen and waste it's sweetness on the desert air.' Well, he was being seen by enough people tonight, he had hardly been off the floor all night.

She mustn't make a fool of herself, she told herself, refusing another glass of wine. After all she wasn't a young one anymore, Still, it was nice to – well – receive attention like this again, and why shouldn't she, there was nothing in the Hippocratic Oath that prohibited dancing with a potential patient at his brother's wedding, not as far as she could recall. As her fourth dance with Petey drew to a close she could see the couple with whom she was to travel home were anxious to leave. She explained the situation to Petey and thanked him for the dances and his company, which, she added, she had enjoyed very much.

'Maybe we could take the floor again before too long,' Petey said, adding hesitantly, 'why don't you drop in for a cup of tea some day?' Her eyes met his .

'Yes –that would be nice, I might just do that sometime–Good night now, Petey.'

'Good night, Molly.'

On Easter Monday Molly drove to Robertstown where she lunched in the small hotel. The area was busy with visitors to the canal-era festival. Afterwards she strolled along the canal path. It was a bright, mild day, with a gentle southerly breeze. Several cruisers and smaller craft were travelling up and down the canal. Spring was all around in the fields. Matronly sheep rested while their lambs larked about, more nimble and frolicsome than they would be ever again in their lives. Along the edges of newly-ploughed fields clusters of furze bushes added a blaze of colour. Small birds sang their hearts out from the hedges, sending signals to potential mates and warnings to rivals to keep off their territory. She wondered what sort of confused signals she sent out to men nowadays. Wouldn't it be better, she thought, if humans were like birds and called out where they stood loudly and clearly?

Nevertheless, she felt much better now, she thought, now that she had reached a decision. She'd drop by on her rounds tomorrow and tell Petey.

She was considering turning back when she saw a familiar figure approaching from the opposite direction. As they drew near she saw, with a considerable start, that it was Petey Horan.

'I've never been here before,' he said, 'I was at this boating festival, or whatever they call it, and I wanted to stretch my legs before I drove home.'

'Something the same for me,' Molly said, 'except I was here years ago, when Arthur was alive. By the way how's Johnny settling in to married life?'

'Oh devil a fear of him – it looks like a case of like a duck to water, if you ask me. You know what they say: 'would you marry a farmer?' Josephine didn't let that put her off anyway! Sure hasn't he the best of care now, with her being a nurse, you know and all that.' he laughed. 'I miss him around the house, though, it's quieter now.'

Molly had a vision – which she quickly dismissed – of Johnny by the fireside, wrapped in the coachman's coat while Josephine, in her nurse's uniform, plied him with his nightly cocoa. There was a pause.

'You never called for that cup of tea, you know, Molly. I was looking forward to that. Did you get that note I sent you?' Petey was watching her closely. Molly hesitated.

'My apologies, Petey, I'm afraid I just didn't get around to it. You see, Petey – I don't know how to put this. The truth is–I've been a bit confused in myself lately – well, you know, actually, I suppose, ever since Arthur died. I really enjoyed the night at the wedding in Athy and dancing with you –and your company, I have to say.'

Petey was staring at her.

'Well – I've decided to retire in two months time In August. I'm going out to Australia to my sister for six months to sort myself out, as it were. Rose and her husband live outside Sydney. They're both retired now and they've invited me to stay as long as I want. I'm sorry if I gave you a wrong impression or if we got our signals crossed – Petey – I just can't–can't make the leap, can't jump this fence, you might say – I think I'm probably a lone bird from here on, somehow, Petey.'

Petey swallowed twice. He hesitated, then asked 'You won't be calling for that cup of tea sometime then?'

'Thanks, but no, Petey, I don't think so,' she said, turning and walking on. 'Goodbye, Petey.'

'Goodbye – Dr Molly.'

He strode off towards Robertstown. He didn't look back. Neither did she.

The End of
the Honeymoon

Alexis Guilbride

Harry gazed gloomily out of his bedroom window at the millions of particles of iced water that frosted the back yard with a cold glistening beauty. The pain in his tooth had kept him awake for most of the night and the freezing temperatures had sharpened the agony. Despite the pain and discomfort, however, he had stayed in the bed, waiting for sleep, instead of getting up to take some pain killers and put a sweater on over his pyjamas. That was typical of him, he thought, angry with himself for his tendency to endure, to wait for his problems to resolve themselves rather than confronting them. He could not put it off any longer. Eva had been right, he would have to go to the dentist.

As he pulled the clothes on over his shivering body he attempted to console himself with a glance at Eva, her plump, rosy body sprawled across the bed semi-naked, as if they were living in the Caribbean, instead of this freezing little artisan's cottage in the Liberties of Dublin. Still, it was their first home. Someday they would like back on it fondly and laugh as they recalled their early hardships in a glow of sentiment. And it was their first rung on the property ladder. He gazed at Eva, waiting for the rush of love and lust he always felt when he watched her sleeping to turn this icy dump into a palace of ardour. Nothing happened. Not a flicker of desire, nothing stirring in the underpants. Well, Harry thought, hardly surprising when the cold has driven your testicles to take refuge in your Adam's apple and you've a raging toothache into the bargain. Nonetheless, he was a little perturbed.

After a spell in the bathroom where he swallowed some aspirin and contemplated brushing his teeth but decided against it, he came back to the bedroom. I won't wake her, he thought, I'll just leave a note. It was Saturday morning and she needed the rest. He scrawled a brief message on the back of an envelope and left it on the bedside table. For a moment he studied his sleeping wife again, and noticed that she hadn't removed her make-up before going to bed last night, and her flushed face was a mess.

Dark clouds hung low and heavy in the swollen sky, threatening snow. Hunched up against the cold, Harry walked briskly down to Whitefriars Street Church. As he passed it he remembered how his mother used to take him there as a boy to get ashes on his forehead on Ash Wednesday and oil on his throat on the Feast of Saint Blaise. That was back in the bad old days before the economic boom, when Dublin was a dark and dirty city, shabby and poor. And yet he remembered it with a degree of warmth and affection, those days when a marshmallow biscuit was the height of luxury, and the ads on Irish television promoted sprays and powders for treating scour and worms in cattle.

Harry wondered, not for the first time, just how much progress had been made since Ireland had become the most globalised economy in the world. There were still beggars in the streets, only now they were Romanian women with hooped earrings and gypsy skirts, and the men selling newspapers on the streets in all weathers were young Africans, instead of old men from the inner city slums. And every day the headlines were the same: yet another shock, horror, terrorist bomb outrage in yet another capital city, in one continent or another, in a world that grew smaller and more fearful every day.

An icy wind off the river howled up Aungier Street and pierced his aching tooth, so that he gasped with pain. Not long now, he moaned to himself, quickening his steps, nearly there. The dental surgery was on the top floor of the Stephen's Green Shopping

Centre. It would probably be busy on a Saturday morning and he didn't have an appointment. He hoped he wouldn't have to wait too long.

A discomfiting thought nagged at the back of his mind and he reached for it with a slight shake of his head. Oh yes, he recalled, Eva, and how her sleeping body had failed to ignite the tiniest spark of desire in him this morning. Was it just his toothache, or was this what people were talking about when they referred to 'the end of the honeymoon'? They had been together for three years now, married for one, and it had never crossed his mind that one day he would grow accustomed to her, no longer find her beautiful. It couldn't happen just like that, surely; if there had been another woman in his thoughts then maybe, but you couldn't just wake up one morning to discover you were no longer in love with your wife, could you?

Police sirens wailed somewhere, growing louder by the moment, seeming to come from all around. Harry looked this way and that, but could not locate the source. Just as the noise rose to brain-scrambling pitch, a team of Garda outriders came hurtling down George's Street, like screaming demons released from the lowest pit of hell, pursued by two black limousines which were in turn followed by another group of outriders. Just as quickly as it had begun, the noise faded away, as cars and riders disappeared in the direction of Dublin Castle. Harry shrugged. Another gang of visiting dignitaries attending the Summit. He still hadn't adjusted to the idea that Ireland was now an important place, and probably never would.

The Ireland of his childhood was insignificant. The Irish had been famous for their hundred thousand welcomes, they were pleased and hospitable when foreigners had deigned to visit them, but a decade of prosperity and State-promoted greed had created instead a nation of raptors whose sharp teeth ripped the cash from the wallets of every tourist foolhardy enough to enter this den of thieves.

He recalled the holidays of his childhood, spent on the Western shores where the local people would greet you in Irish as you wandered the little winding roads in the clear air and there was nothing to fear but the sea. Today it was all traffic jams and cafes serving hazelnut lattes at incredibly inflated prices, and other people, potential muggers, rapists, child molesters, even, God forbid, terrorists, were far more frightening than the elements. The native tongue had been jettisoned by the State, it had no market value, after all. Even Yeats, railing against the shopkeeper mentality of the newly-independent State, fingers fumbling in greasy tills, could not have anticipated this particular outrage.

All that mattered now were more cars, more coffee and more choice. But somehow Harry felt he had fewer and fewer choices, these days. He was one of the lucky ones, he knew that. In a time when ever-increasing numbers found themselves homeless and living on the streets, he owned a house. That is to say, the bank owned the house, and they owned him too. And with that thought the realisation dawned that it wasn't his wife that he had fallen out of love with, it was his life, his town, his country, his world. Everything that he had known and loved was gone, like his childhood, and something ugly had taken its place. Maybe that was it, maybe he was just getting old. But, godammit, he was only thirty-four. He was too young to be old. For a moment he felt a sense of empathy with the suicide bombers and the anarchists, with their 'destroy everything' mentality. Maybe it was time to blow it all up and start again.

He had reached the entrance to the shopping centre and he had to tack his way through the milling crowds that already thronged this cathedral of consumerism. A faint recollection stirred in him, a flashback to his early childhood. His mother used to bring him with her to this place occasionally on a Saturday morning, in the days when it was the Dandelion Market, a ramshackle collection of stalls where hippies sold second-hand clothes and home-made carrot cake, an Aladdin's cave of wonderment. All changed, changed utterly. He had Yeats on the brain. All he wanted now was to get his tooth fixed and get home to Eva. He would take her in his arms and kiss her grubby face and tell her that he loved her, she was all that he lived for.

He was halfway up the escalator to the first floor when a blinding light seemed to set his eyeballs on fire and a searing pain ripped through his whole body. For a moment of infinite agony time stood still, and mangled bodies seemed to hang in the air around him, motionless. Then Harry felt himself falling, the great blast of noise that had shattered his eardrums diminishing, fading with the fading light into silence and darkness and oblivion.

Eva reached lazily across the bed, searching for Harry's warm body, her eyes still closed. Not finding it she awoke with a sense of anxiety and caught sight of the note on the bedside table.

'Gone to the Dentist, I'll call you as soon as I know how long it's likely to take. Love you, Harry.'

Ambulance sirens wailed in the streets outside, but they made no impact on her consciousness. She was safe and warm and happy. She snuggled down under the duvet and smiled contentedly, stroking her stomach lovingly with both hands. When she did the Home Pregnancy Test last night after they came home from the party, she wanted to tell Harry there and then that it had come out positive, but he was sound asleep by the time she came out of the bathroom. She had hesitated for a moment, then realised she couldn't wake him, it wouldn't be fair. He had been in so much pain. And a Home Pregnancy Test was no guarantee anyway, although somehow she knew it was right, she could feel it. Never mind, she thought, I'll tell him in the morning.

The Showing

Arthur Sheridan

They carried the stuff down to the van. None of them really understood Steo's art, or any art for that matter, except Rapper. And he was strange anyway. As they re-entered the flat, the music of Bob Marley pulsed off the walls at a volume that hurt the ears. Elvis was king to most people, but to Steo, that throne was reserved for Marley. Posters of the Jamaican hero covered the wall, and Steo sometimes talked to them, looking for inspiration.

Struggling with a large item, he called Rapper to help. Rapper, dressed in a black shiny tracksuit and baseball cap, squatted down over a coffee table, absorbed in some arty photographs and the rap music which played on his Walkman. Steo, realizing that Rapper couldn't hear him over both musics asked: 'What'd he bring his little brother with him for?'

'He thought he might be a help,' said Johner.

'Where's he now?' asked Steo.

'Dropping a log,' Johner said.

'Every time there's work to be done your man hides in the bog,' Steo said, getting annoyed.

'That's why we call him Boggo,' grinned Johner.

A flushing noise entered the room along with Boggo. He looked around while tucking his shirt in his jeans.

'Have yiz not got the stuff loaded yet?' he asked.

'No,' said Steo.

'This one's heavy. Gi's a hand with it.'

They struggled down the stairs with the piece. Women with shopping stopped and children stared, wondering what the hell they were staring at. Two wooden arses bet into one another, one with barbed wire stuck in it. Rapper sauntered down the stairs and watched them load it in the van.

'Well, that's the lot,' said Steo.

'Did you lock up?' he asked Rapper.

Rapper stared at the arses in the van, still unable to hear above the Walkman. Steo walked up the steps, annoyed at not being heard, and mumbling something about when wanting something done right.

He stood in the doorway and surveyed the flat. Bob Marley still incoming on the Stereo. He looked at the paint stains and the hardened pieces of modelling clay. The dust from plaster of paris and the smell of solvents from paints and resins. And the remaining pieces. Ten years of work in his flat, he thought to himself. All his hopes and dreams, sparked by a night course on art, years earlier. And today was the moment of truth. Make or break time. The showing. He thought of all the work and time he'd put in. Of his thirtieth birthday, which loomed closer. He couldn't fail now. He just had to make it. For weeks he'd been fighting the fear of rejection, which was growing stronger. It was a struggle to control the pressure which was building inside him. He looked at the furniture. He'd built it all himself from wooden pallets. He'd seen the idea in a magazine article. He was proud of them at first. But after the lads had slagged them, one night after the pub, he'd started to feel disappointed in them. His pride was restored when he saw something similar on a television show. Futons me arse, he'd thought. They're just fancy pallets. He turned off the stereo, removed the tape and put it in his pocket. Bob would take his mind off his worries. He locked and returned to the van.

'Okay lads, time to head,' he said.

He swung the van out of the car park, the four boys squashed in front. They drove onto the main road and headed for the other side of the city. Steo stuck the tape in the deck and hit a button. The music lightened the mood. Three of them rocked side to side to the rhythm of reggae singing 'Jamming'. The other stared out the window. His lips moving slightly to the rap music on the Walkman.

Things were buzzing at the exhibition hall when they arrived. Everyone else was set up already.

'You're late', said the organiser, 'it starts at eleven.'

'It's only quarter to now,' said Steo.

Most of the stands are gone, but there may be one left beside the toilets,' the organiser said. The lads humped the articles through the crowds. They passed a woman looking at bright splashes on canvas.

'I like that one,' she said to a friend. 'What would be the right setting for it?'

'A very dark room,' Boggo shouted back at her. They disappeared into the crowd, Johner and Boggo laughing. Steo looked vexed. He felt let down by their juvenile humour.

What would his fellow artists think?

They set the pieces on the stall. The arses seemed to raise a few eyebrows, but not the organizers who'd probably seen it all before. Steo thought how out of the way the stall was. He'd hoped to get a good spot.

'Where's the bar?' asked Boggo.

'There's no bar,' said Steo.

'Then what do we drink?' asked the lads, looking worried.

'There's a refreshment stall over there, they have tea, coffee and wine,' said Steo.

And that's when he saw her. Standing with a glass of wine. Looking cool. Almost cold. Dark shoulder length hair. Dark eyes. Lips unsmiling. Almost pouting. Long slender legs. Her slim figure wrapped in a boob tube and short lycra skirt. A buffalo girl hat on her head. He wanted to approach her. To tell her of his attraction. But he couldn't do that. What could he use as an opening line? How could he play down the obvious? Maybe the attraction wasn't mutual. Maybe she'd turn him down. Or maybe she'd just walk away, ignoring him completely, like he didn't exist. God I'd hate that, he thought. I'd really hate that.

'She's a cracker,' he heard Boggo say.

He noticed everyone looking to his right and turned to see what they were looking at. The judges were approaching. He felt the pressure building up inside him. His heart raced, his mouth dried, and his tongue felt alien and oversized in his mouth. The judges looked at his stand, trying to ignore the arses, but their eyes kept going back to them involuntarily.

'What's that one about?' one of them asked, pointing to a model of Ireland with a pie coming out of it, and a man standing on it with a suitcase in one hand and two fingers raised back at the country. The whole thing painted snot green.

'It's about, sorta, the way the unemployed feel, like, when they have to emigrate, you know.' The judges looked unimpressed.

'It's the rape of the nation. A betrayed generation, a country's 'greatest asset' preparing for their exportation,' rapped Rapper.

Steo stared at Rapper, looking baffled and pleasantly surprised. He had said what Steo was trying to say the way Steo would have liked to say it. This man has soul, thought Steo. Everyone else stared at Rapper just baffled.

'What's he on about?' asked Johner.

'Ah he's bleedin mad,' said Boggo. 'Lets have some of the wine.'

The judges moved on. Steo turned towards the refreshment stall but she was gone. He went looking at the other exhibits, keeping an eye out for her, but she'd disappeared. Rapper looked at a few exhibits then disappeared too. Johner and Boggo spent all their time at the refreshment stall, drinking wine. The judges, having seen all the works, started their deliberations. Steo felt his heartbeat quicken and his stomach heave slightly. The tension was killing him. He could feel a migraine coming on. A migraine, he thought to himself. A fuckin' migraine. Migraines are for accountants. What's happening to me? He turned and looked at Johner and Boggo. Maybe the lads have the right idea, he thought. He joined them at the refreshments stand. The wine numbed him a bit, though he could still feel the tension inside him. The judges were handing out the prizes, of which there were many, starting with the lowest and working their way up.

'Looks like there's one for everyone in the audience,' laughed Boggo. Occasionally he and Johner sniggered at a piece. Steo listened to the judges. Hanging on their every word. Waiting for a mention of his name. The pressure building higher. It came to first prize. Steo's name not mentioned yet. His hopes and spirits raised. This could be it. This could be his moment.

'And the winner is… Dorian Finerty, for her lovely still life flowers.' The moment collapsed as someone else's name was called out. His life crashed all around him. He struggled to control the pain. He grabbed two glasses of wine and headed towards the door. As he left he heard the beginning of the organizer's speech.

'We'd like to thank everyone who entered works, most of which were bright and cheerful.' It stung. It stung hard.

Steo sat into the cab of the van where he found Rapper.

'I lost,' he confided, 'Nothing. Not a dickie bird.' He sipped the wine trying to cope with the depression. 'It's not the winning,' he said. 'That's not what was important. I was looking for something. Anything, a sign. Something to tell me that I hadn't wasted my time. That the last ten years weren't for nothing.' He turned and looked at Rapper. Rapper still listening to his Walkman hadn't heard a word. The pressure soared and Steo blew a headgasket.

His anger and tension flooded out. He slammed the door, storming of in a huff. Rapper, feeling the movement, turned and looked, but seeing nobody there went back to his music and daydreaming.

Steo walked and sipped, then hopped on the Dart. He sat, watching youngsters laughing and joking, heading out for the night. His bitterness and disappointment were pushing him. 'Why don't yiz shut the fuck up, yiz noisy bastards,' he roared, jumping to his feet. They sat there in quiet fear, staring at him, then turned away, afraid to look.

'He's a crazy looking bastard,' he heard someone whisper. A murmuring started and everyone stared at the nut. Steo just sat there, looking out the window, sipping and festering. The empty glasses rolled around the seat and clinked as he hopped from the Dart and headed for the off-licence. He took a cheap bottle of sherry and a two litre of wine from a shelf, paid, and headed out the door and into the noise. This should do the job, he thought to himself.

Johner turned to Boggo looking bored and slightly worried. 'I don't think he's coming back,' he said. They looked into the hall. The crowd now gone, tables folded and stacked and butts everywhere. One stall remained with Steo's work on it. The organiser gave the lads an impatient stare. 'Well, I suppose we better load it in the van,' said Johner. They beckoned Rapper to help. 'Not like Steo to go off like that,' Johner said, looking concerned.

"No, not like him,' agreed Boggo.' Maybe he's clicked a woman.'

'Nah, don't think so,' said Johner.

Van loaded, they started the journey home. But didn't' get very far when they had to stop for Boggo to pee. Johner felt the effects of the wine soon after and it was his turn to stop the van. And so they went on, alternating all the way home.

'Could yiz not both pee at the same time,' said Rapper getting pissed off with it all.

'A man gotta go when a man gotta go,' said Boggo in a John Wayne voice. The two boys laughed. Rapper stared out the window and turned up the volume on his Walkman.

Steo was well gone when he entered the flat. The wine drank, he started on the sherry. He stared at the contents of the room and then in a blaze of fury kicked an empty paint can across the floor. 'Load of shite,' he screamed. Materials, pictures, even his furniture, everything suffered the wrath of his boot. Then he noticed the giant piece of canvas. A discarded truck cover someone had given him. He'd spent weeks bleaching it in the bath, trying to get it ready for painting. Crazy thoughts came into his head. 'Bright and cheerful. I'll give ye bright and fuckin' cheerful,' he screamed, trying to hold back the tears.

Standing on the roof of the flats he could see the canvas on the pavement below where he'd left it, weighted at the corners with a glass ashtray and some modeling clay. He took a swig from the sherry bottle. He thought of the art competition. Bright splashes on canvas. He thought of all the slaggings he'd got over the years about his stuff. He thought of all the putdowns he'd had from his parents, his teachers, neighbours, and girlfriends.

'Fuck the bleedin' lot of yiz,' he shrieked. Me final work, he thought.

'Artists never make it till they're dead,' Boggo had once told him.

'We'll fuckin' see now,' he shrieked. He gulped some sherry and then, suddenly, the air was filled with the sound of Bob Marley. It wrestled his desire to jump. A sudden light was hurting his eyes. On the balcony below a door had just opened and he spied creamy, white breasts in a boob tube. She looked up at him. Her face coming out from under the buffalo girl hat.

'Hi. What're you doing up there?' she asked. Steo was stunned.

'Eh, getting some air and watching the stars,' he stammered.

'But it's cloudy,' she replied. She lit the biggest joint Steo had ever seen and offered it to him. He lowered himself onto the balcony.

'I saw you at the art exhibition today,' he said, trying to make conversation.

'So I noticed,' she said.

'I really liked your stuff. It was very good.'

'Did ye really?' asked Steo, his spirit brightening.

'Yeah. Those judges didn't understand art,' she said. 'They chose pieces like they were picking wallpaper or something.'

This woman has great taste, thought Steo.

'How come I haven't seen you around before?' he asked.

I've been away for the last four years, studying art in Paris,' she answered, 'I know some people over there that might be interested in your work.' His confidence soared. That was it, he realised. The sign he'd hoped for. He hadn't been wasting his time. There was a purpose to life. The mixture of dope and booze made everything seem unreal. Did I jump and am now in heaven, he wondered. 'No Woman No Cry' played on the stereo.

'I love that song,' she said. 'Do you like Marley?'

'Like him! He's my inspiration,' said Steo. She took the sherry from Steo's hand and put it on the floor, then

kissed him. She's not backward about coming forward, he thought. Maybe there is a god after all. They slow danced together.

'Thank you,' he said quietly. 'Thank you, Saint Bob.'

The lads pulled up on the street below to see them kissing.

'There he is up there,' said Boggo. 'See. I told you he'd clicked a woman.' He turned to Johner.

'And you getting us all worried.' Something else had caught Johner's eye. 'Look at that tarpaulin over there,' he said.

I bet Steo could use that.'

'Stick it in the back of the van,' said Boggo. The three lads climbed out of the van.

Rapper stretched his stiff legs.

I'm bursting for a leak,' Boggo said.

I'm off home,' said Rapper, annoyed at Boggo for mentioning pee again.

'You can go in the Oak. It's not closing time yet,' said Johner.

'Your man can unload his own stuff. He has a spare set of keys.'

'Too right,' said Boggo. The lads locked the van and headed down the road for some proper drink and some serious bladder relieving.

Growing Up

Joe O'Reilly

Pat is me mate from way back. Some people say he is a loudmouth and not to be trusted but I like him. He's a bit older than me and me Ma doesn't like him. 'That boy is a bad lot. He thinks of no one but himself. He's far too smarmy for my liking,' she says. In any case this holiday was all his idea.

'Tim, I'm thinking of going abroad this year.' We were in the tennis club sitting near the court that we had booked where four young women were playing a spirited game. I was watching their every move, every service, every bend, every stretch – and trying to imagine what tennis must be like in a nudist colony. Reluctantly I pulled my eyes away.

'I can't afford it, Pat. You know that. Auld Doyle pays buttons until you're qualified and that won't be until next year. It's all right for you with your job, – and you don't have to give your Ma anything.'

'Think about it, Tim.' He persisted. 'Sun, sand and maybe sex. It doesn't cost as much as you think. I have a brochure. It doesn't have to be dear at all.' He went on and on.

That was how it all started. It seems a long time ago now. The brochure fired my imagination. The blue sea, the beautiful beaches, those women with the microscopic bikinis, that place Mont. St. Michel with all the steps, those women in bikinis... I wavered for a few days but finally agreed. We settled – or at least

Pat settled on – St. Malo, a place in France. The money I scraped together, first the deposit and finally the balance, this with the aid of a loan from my father – not lightly given I can tell you.

It was only the day before we left that Pat let slip that Olivia and a pal of hers had booked the same tour and would be staying at the same hotel. Pat was a bit vague about the pal. He thought her name was Margaret but he wasn't sure. I knew Olivia, of course. Pat was mad about her. She wasn't a bad-looking bird but she hadn't a brain in her head. I wasn't sure how she felt but according to Pat she couldn't live without him. But I didn't know any Margaret. Pat was offhand as if it didn't matter but I was annoyed. It did matter and he should have told me. I didn't relish the idea of being stuck with someone I had never met for six days and what worried me more was the nights. What had he in mind? 'Nothing,' Pat said with injured innocence. I pressed the question. 'We'll take it if it is on offer but only if.' He tried to calm me. Nothing would happen unless I wanted it to happen. All I had to do was be nice to her and give Olivia and himself some space.

It was my first time on a plane and I was glad when we got there I can tell you. My stomach was uneasy for the whole flight. Although she must have been on the plane we didn't see Olivia until we landed. She greeted us as if she had come a thousand miles to meet us and drooled over Pat who in turn licked her ear. Disgusting. She introduced Margaret and I found my opinion on the holiday was changing. She was a dish. Short black hair, lively brown eyes, a good figure, nay a magnificent figure, that defied me to look at anything else. Margaret was warm and friendly and laughed easily. I knew straightaway I was going to like her. But the two girls sat together on the bus on our way to St. Malo.

The first day we spent exploring the old walled town and the immediate neighbourhood. I found myself alone with Margaret a lot of the time. Pat and Olivia seemed to fade into the background at odd moments leaving the two of us to get to know each other and the more I got to know her the more I liked her.

She had a ready sense of humour and took a joke well. But what I liked most was the way she stood close to me without appearing to notice. Most of the girls I knew kept their distance. I was sure she felt comfortable with me.

It was the evening of the second day and Pat and myself were getting ready to go out to dinner.

'How are you getting on with Margaret? She's a great looking bird, isn't she?' For the fourth time Pat combed his hair and tousled it to get the effect he wanted.

I gave my man-of-the-world laugh. 'I wouldn't charge her anything, that's for sure.'

'She thinks you're something special too, so Olivia says. Will we try it to-night then? You can go to their room and Olivia will come up here.'

'If things go okay,' I murmured and felt something like an electric current going through me.

That night at dinner we did in a bottle of red and a bottle of white. As soon as the meal was over I found myself looking at Margaret speculatively. Would she or wouldn't she? But suddenly she stood up and laid her hand firmly on Olivia's shoulder.

'Come on, my girl. The wine is going to your head. You'll be doing a hornpipe on the table soon.' She laughed but nevertheless marched Olivia firmly out of the restaurant before Pat could think of a suitable delaying tactic. He muttered 'shit' several times. To be honest I felt disappointed and relieved at the same time, if you know what I mean.

That night I dreamt of Margaret in those grey trousers that she wore, and then there was that bikini ... Funnily enough when I awoke money was the first thing I thought of. Although we split everything four ways I was spending far more than I had budgeted for. I would have to talk to Pat.

That day there was an air of suppressed excitement between the four of us. I knew why. We took a bus tour to Mont St. Michel. It is a fabulous place and we all enjoyed it. But I decided this would have to be my last tour. These tours were too expensive. As dinnertime approached the tension increased. I dressed with extra care. Pat was in front of the mirror at his hair again.

'I hope you're ready for anything to-night, Tim. Olivia will come up here. Margaret has agreed, too. She and you can have the girls' room. It's all plain sailing from here on in.'

I choked. 'I don't think she'd agree.'

'Margaret? Don't be daft, Tim. She's mad for it. You can take Olivia's word for that. Every time they're alone she's talking about you. You have only to ask, I promise you.' Pat waved the hairbrush at me. 'At the right time I'll suggest it and all you have to do is look at Margaret and say you're game.'

We dawdled over dinner. Olivia sluiced down the white as if it were going out of fashion. When the coffee came I felt the moment of decision had arrived and glanced at Pat. But suddenly Margaret stood up. 'I'm not feeling well, all of a sudden. In fact I think I'm going to get sick. I have to go to bed. Don't break it up on my account.' But, of course, it did break it up. Olivia became all concern and left with her. I was disappointed. Pat muttered something that I couldn't catch and lapsed into a sulky silence. I knew better than to talk.

That night I counted what was left of my money. I counted it again. I couldn't have spent so much in three days. I did a review. Yes, it was about right. It was the dinners – and the wine, and two bottles every night! I would have been happy with a one-and-one or a Big Mac or even a single course and at most a glass of wine. I could afford one more night of this and after that I would have to go on a diet of fresh air.

Breakfast on the morning of the fourth day. Margaret seemed totally recovered. She was wearing those tight grey trousers again. She had decided that she wanted to go to Dinan. She had been reading the tourist bumf and ranted on for a bit about it. It was an old cathedral town. Pat wasn't enthusiastic. 'It's too nice a day. Let's hit the beach. I want to see the bikinis.' He suggested and Olivia rowed in behind him. We decided to explore the walled town in the morning and to spend the afternoon on the beach. I heaved a sigh of relief. That was at least a €100 saved. I would have to borrow a few shekels from Pat but now I could wait until to-morrow.

It was on the beach or rather in the sea that Margaret confided in me. 'Have you noticed,' she asked me when I came up for air. 'Pat is trying to get Olivia into bed.' I gulped as my mind raced trying to understand what she was saying. Clear thinking was difficult as she seemed to be leaning against me for support. I looked ashore to where Pat and Olivia were deep in conversation. 'He doesn't know it but he's wasting his time. She likes him well enough. It's just that she doesn't want to hurry things.'

'I – I thought that they had already ...' My voice died.

'No, they haven't. She's not that sort of girl.' She said this firmly. 'This holiday was not her idea, you know. We had booked and when Pat heard it he booked as well. I didn't know anything about it until the morning we were leaving.'

'But she was ready to go with him last night. In fact I was wondering what you and I were going to do.' I murmured finding her close presence very exciting.

'Hmmm That's an interesting thought,' she put her arms around me and for an instant I thought we were going to do it where we stood. 'But this is not the time. We can explore it when we get home. Right now we have to help Olivia to keep Pat at arm's length. Don't say it to him, of course. She doesn't want to hurt his feelings.'

So Olivia was the problem. My mind was in turmoil. This holiday was turning out better than I expected. I put my arms around her and kissed her there in the water. She responded warmly and then set off for the shore.

That evening much to Pat's surprise as soon as I had dressed I announced that I was going for a short walk. 'But don't wait for me. I know where to find you,' I said curtly to him making it clear that I didn't want company. In fact I didn't want to talk to him in case he would notice the confusion in my mind.

And that was how it happened. As I walked down a narrow

street in the town a figure a good distance ahead of me stooped
to tie his shoelace. I paid little attention but noted absently that
the man was well dressed. The street was deserted – that hour
before dinner. He had been hurrying and as I came up to him he
straightened and raced ahead again. Suddenly I saw a wallet
lying just where he had been. I picked it up and raised my hand
to call him but was just in time to see him turn the corner at the
end of the street. It was a fat wallet. I glanced inside. There was
a wad of money in €50s and €20s, probably about €600 in all.
All my problems were solved. My mind ran riot. Pat and Olivia
could have dinner on their own. I would invite Margaret to a
special dinner with lots of wine. Afterwards we would stroll
hand-in-hand – What was I thinking of? I couldn't keep this
money. It wasn't mine. It would lie on my conscience, spoil my
enjoyment of the rest of the holiday. Even if Margaret said 'yes'
to a roll in the hay it would not be worth it. Well, maybe it
would. I thought of her bikini-clad figure again. No, no, no.
There was only one way of dealing with this. I would have to
give it back. I hurried forward around the corner where the man
had disappeared. This street was wider. I examined the dozen or
so people in sight but my man was not among them. I raced on
down the street to the corner. There I caught a glimpse of him
just going through the big gate.

I saw him nip smartly across the road leading to St. Servan. I
followed waiting for a gap in the traffic so that I could cross. He
turned into a side street. Finally I got across. I hurried to the
side street and looked. No sign of him. I raced along that street,
turned left and then right. I went on for a while but eventually
had to admit defeat. He was gone.

Well, it wasn't all bad. I could now keep the money with a
clear conscience. No one could have done more. I counted it
carefully. €640, to be exact. It would be pointless giving it to the
police. The amount was too small. I turned to make my way
back. It was then I saw the two thugs. I tried to run but one of
them grabbed my collar and hit me hard in the face. They were
yelling at me in French. I decided the end had come and closed

my eyes. But just then I heard another shout and suddenly the thugs were gone. I opened my eyes. The whole thing had probably taken only a few seconds but it felt like a year.

My saviours were two young guys built like tanks. They descended on me talking French excitedly. I tried to thank them. Finally they calmed down and led me back to a busy street. We shook hands and they left. My eye was beginning to feel sore. It was a while before I realised I had no idea where I was.

It was after nine before I got to familiar surroundings. I bought something in a takeaway and retired to the hotel to eat it. There was no sense in seeking the others out now. Olivia was not up for it and I wasn't feeling great myself. I was in bed when Pat arrived.

'Where the Hell were you? I was worried. I was going to go to the police.' Then he caught sight of me. 'Jesus, what happened to you?'

I gave him a short account of the night's events omitting any mention of the money. I thought it better to say nothing about it. He listened attentively. 'Olivia was agreeable tonight, damn it. We had it all readied up. But we couldn't ditch Margaret with you not there. Damn it, Tim, this holiday is turning into a bad dream.' Then as an afterthought. 'I better tell the girls you're all right.' He lifted the phone and I heard his account and felt like wrenching the phone from him to put matters right.

The fifth day. I went through my adventure again over breakfast. The girls were impressed. It was almost worth the black eye. Later Margaret mentioned Dinan again. I said nothing. So we went on another bus tour – fiendishly expensive. 'One more night to keep Olivia out of Pat's clutches.' Margaret murmured grimly to me as we mounted the bus for the return journey. I had thought of that too but I wasn't so sure. Every time I looked at them they seemed to be wrapped up in each other. In my opinion Margaret and myself could have stripped off on the spot and the pair wouldn't have noticed. Now there's a thought!

Dinner that night was low key. We knew it was our last night.

We dallied over the food but finally we paid the bill and made our way out into the balmy night. 'Let's go for a walk. It's a beautiful night and it is our last.' This from Margaret.

We sauntered along the seafront, Margaret and I leading the way. I slipped my arm around her and she leaned in to me. Everywhere had become quiet. I glanced behind but there was no sign of Pat and Olivia. Taking her by surprise I pointed her across the street and pulled her into a doorway. We wrapped our arms around each other and kissed. It was only then that she realised that Pat and Olivia were not with us. Straightaway she became anxious. 'Let's go back, Tim. It's too quiet here. I don't feel comfortable.' We turned for the hotel and I could hardly keep up with her.

We found Pat and Olivia in earnest conversation in the foyer. We joined them but Margaret seemed overcome with tiredness. She yawned several times and then said: 'I've had it. I'm off to bed. Are you coming, Olivia?' Suddenly she was gone. Olivia turned to Pat and made a face and then she, too, was gone. Pat used foul language and included the three of us in his cursing. I said nothing.

The journey home was uneventful. I had to give a censored version of the holiday to my parents. My father was reassured when I gave him back €200. He said I could forget about the rest.

In the week that followed I found Pat very hard to contact. He wasn't in the tennis club nor did I meet him at swimming. I rang the number Margaret had given me but she wasn't there. Each time her mother took the message but nothing happened. I tried again and again. I began to feel like a leper.

It was more than a week later that I met Olivia. I felt it was not by chance. She might have been waiting to catch me on my way home from work. The minute she saw me she burst out. 'Did you know Pat and Margaret spent the weekend together in Kilkenny?' There were tears in her voice. I caught my breath. 'The night after we came home Margaret confided in me that Pat had tried it on with her every time he got her alone but that she hadn't said anything because she didn't want to spoil the holiday. Anyway I threw it at him when we met. He denied it, of course; said he was just being friendly. We ended up having a flaming row. The next thing I hear is this. I – I can't believe it.' She burst into tears. I put my arms around her. What else could I do?

I could see now what Margaret had been after all along. But what could I say. After all Pat is me mate. I held Olivia tightly until the sobbing stopped. If things were right I could go for her. She's a nice girl really.

Forbidden Love

Michael P. McCormack

'Rachel! Rachel!' he screamed at the top of his lungs.

'She'll be here shortly son; I've done my bit now, how about releasing one of the guards?' a calm voice asked from the other side of the door.

'Rachel… Rachel' he yelled again only louder this time.

'Why don't you put that silly thing away son, I'm sure we could settle this all out over a nice cuppa,' the voice said again.

'If you don't bring Rachel down in the next five minutes I'll slit one of der poxy throats,' he screamed and,to show them outside he wasn't messing about, he grabbed one of the young gardai he was holding captive up by the hair, placed the hunting knife across his throat, then nicked his hostage just enough to convince them outside that he meant business.

'Listen, she'll be here shortly, just don't do anything stupid son,' the voice pleaded from outside the door.

Garda Gerry Mc Niffe and his colleague Garda Tom Chaney were trussed up like two chickens in the hallway of the second storey corporation flat complex of the North Circular Road. It was Gerry who spoke now:

'Listen Stan, I really think you should free Tom, 'he whispered,' thankful that their captor was still half reasonable.

'I don't think so,' he mimicked, walking over and slapping Chaney across the face.

'Stan, this is way too personal for you,' Gerry whispered in his soft country brogue.

'Dis cunt here,' he said, kicking at Chaney 'visited Rachel's ma last night. Mrs fucking Dunne starts calling me a rapist and a child molester, she refuses to let me see her daughter; now work it out,' he moaned, lashing out now at Chaney's legs.

'Listen Stan, maybe it's just a mix up, I'm sure between me, you and Mrs Dunne we can sort this out,' Gerry whispered hoping to calm the situation down a peg or two.

'Don't mind that dirty, murdering, raping scumbag. He's going to the Hill with the rest of the sex cases,' Chaney spit in the direction of his captor.

'Tom, for fucksake man, cut that shite out will you,' he hushed slightly, raising the tone of his voice in condemnation at his fellow officer and captive.

'Dis is what dis is all about isn't it; Chaney there couldn't catch me so him and that auld gee-bag Mrs Dunne decided to stitch me up,' he muttered. Walking over to Chaney he viciously stamped on the garda's groin sending him rolling around the floor in pain.

'Stan this is going way too far son, you really have to ease up,' Gerry whispered realising he was losing control of the situation; not that he had any control at all but Tom could be a bit more diplomatic instead, of aggravating the kid.

'How old is Rachel?' Gerry enquired.

'She's only fifteen, dirty Mickey there raped her," Chaney spit out.

He walked down the hallway returned and pretended to kick Chaney in the chest, stopping short by less than an inch.

'Dis fucker better shut up, Gerry,' he said agitated, waving his finger in the direction of Chaney whom was suddenly starting to look the worse for wear.

'You're going to kill him Stan, then all of the others who come running through the door are going to want a piece of you,' Gerry whispered nodding towards the door.

'Rachel's going to have our baby, she's sixteen in a couple of weeks time, why couldn't we be left a-fucking-lone,' he muttered to nobody in particular.

Gerry took it that the boy wanted this to end.

'You give me the knife and I'll walk you out, I promise you Stan. No, I give you me word Stan, that I will talk up for you. If there is any underhanded stuff going on between Chaney and Mrs Dunne I'll bring it to the relevant bodies,' he whispered, hoping that the boy would take the carrot.

'Gerry, stop trying to give the little pervert hope,' Chaney spluttered.

'Rachel....' he screamed out again.

The voice was back from outside the door,

'She'll be here in a few minutes son; your mammy is here and very anxious to see you son, shall I tell her you're willing to talk to her,' the negotiator offered.

'Course I'll talk to her she's me ma you fucking idiot,' he said after the disappearing go-between.

Brigit Camac was well into her fifties. She had two living children from six pregnancies, the other four resulting in stillborns. Her husband Archie had gone missing shortly after the birth of her last baby, Thurstan. On hearing he was going to be a father again, Archibald Camac, before heading to the nearest pub to wet his new born baby son's head had dropped into the local bookies. Where he did a $1 Yankee, across the board, all long shots. The shortest price winner he had was a 33 to 1 shot, the longest was a 100 to 1 shot. Archie Camac walked from the bookies a rich man and subsequently disappeared off the face of the earth. Brigit, on the other hand, had to rear her newborn and his four-year-old sister, Tracey. To make ends meet she worked in a shop during the morning and did a bit of sewing at night. Her prospects in life only started to take a turn for the better when her children left school and began to work. Tracey was a machinist and Thurstan was a labourer, both working locally. But something in that boy courted trouble; he had been let go over an argument with his boss. The following week his boss ended up in hospital with broken arms and legs. The boss's jeep, along with his house, went on fire very mysteriously too. Thurstan forever pleading the innocent received a three-year prison sentence. They had let him out in June of this year and less than two months later he was back in trouble.

'Are you alright son?' she asked through her own hall door.

'I'm sorry, ma about the place, I promise to get things fixed up when I get this trouble sorted,' he offered.

'It's only glass and wood son, it could be a lot worse, it could be blood and bones,' she whispered.

He smiled at her knowing that she always looked on the bright side of things, forever the optimist.

'They say they can sort this mess out if you let the two policemen go about their business,' she said.

'Listen Ma the only people who can sort this out is me and Rachel,' he replied.

'That Rachel, she's a nice girl. I really thought you would've settled down with her,' his mother added.

'Dat's what this trouble is all about Ma, so if you head down to Mary's I'll be down shortly,' he whispered calmly.

'Well you just be careful,' she whispered and turned to walk away; she stopped halfway down the balcony and returned to her hall door,

'Tell me everything is going to be alright son,' she whispered into the letterbox.

'Ma! I love you, y' know everything's going to be ok; you slip down to Old Mary's and have that cup of rosy. Before your finished I'll be sitting beside you,' he said with a smile and he blew her a kiss through the door.

'Ok son,' she sighed, turning away from her hall door, tears began rolling down her cheeks. Brigit Camac sensed there was something wrong with this night, deep down some maternal instinct warned her that this very night her boy would be gone forever. She felt her weary heart miss a beat as she slowly descended the stairs.

'Ye know all I ever wanted was to be left alone, I mean our baby's due in two weeks time. Rachel's sixteen soon, please god she'll be a mother, I've already the deposit for a flat, why all of a sudden is the shit hitting the fucking fan? Why?' he muttered loudly.

Something deep down inside Gerry Mc Niffe's psyche heard alarm bells ringing, he sensed a vital lifeline being thrown.

'Listen Stan you can have it all, son, if you want; ok, so she's a little bit young but even I find it hard sometimes to tell the difference between ages. But this issue here is much more serious. If you want to see your baby grow up you have a choice to make. If you don't end this now your child will remember seeing its father in prison until way past its communion. Listen to me, Stan, for everybody's sake let it go, son, give it up now,' he whispered, knowing the sound of his soft country brogue was turning the drama that was unfolding around them into some sort of surreal crappy advertisement for Ovaltine.

'Don't be feeling sorry for that fucking child molester, he's going were he belongs with the rest of the scum, Arbour Hill' Chaney chided.

'Rachel…' he screamed again.

'You want to learn to shut that mouth of yours, Tom, before he really goes to work on you' Gerry whispered, inwardly wishing he could give Chaney a good hiding for aggravating the situation.

'She's on her way up the stairs,' the negotiator said through the door and vanished as quickly as he had appeared. He could hear her talking to somebody as she made her way up the balcony. When she finally arrived at the door he realised by the sound of her voice that she was terrified.

'You're going to have to come out,' she said, shivering through the tears that were flowing silently down her face.

'What the fuck is going on?' he asked. Before she could reply her mother was grabbing her away from the door and shouting to the onlookers that; that bastard in there raped her poor little Rachel and if she had her way she'd let the guards shoot the fucker.

'What's going on, Rachel? I though you wanted to be with me,' he called, as she wrestled free from her mother's reins.

'I love you Stan, but my mother said she'll cast me out onto the street if I don't disown you,' she cried.

'Well that's it then, isn't it?' he whispered, the tears streaming down his face.

'I do love you Stan but I've nowhere to go,' she cried.

'You can live with me,' he pleaded.

'Stan you're going to prison, Chaney told me I'd belong to the social services until I'm eighteen. My mother called me a retard, what am I to do? I have no one to turn to" she trailed off. She began to cry hysterically.

'Dat's it then, love,' he whispered watching her turn away and into her mother's arms. He could barely see her walk down the balcony and out of his sight forever. In the distance he could hear her mother yelling that her daughter would never bring a bastard into the world. That she would be on the ferry in the morning. He sagged down on bended knees and closed his eyes to the world and the mess he was in. He was brought back by the sound of Gerry Mc Niffe's voice.

'Listen Stan, you got to bring this to an end now, you have my word that I'll help you in anyway I can but end it now, son.'

'Yeah, rapist, end it now,' Chaney sniggered.

He dried the last remaining tears from his face, grabbed Chaney by the hair and began by smacking his head constantly off the toilet door. Whispering into the garda's face he asked;

'Besides breathing what have I done to deserve this special treatment from you?'

Chaney smirked through his bloodied mouth and muttered, 'Fucking joy-riders, you all deserve to die.'

'Jesus Stan, let it go he's only a fucking arsehole,' Gerry whispered, as it suddenly dawned on him what was happening. A stolen car had killed Chaney's parents about eighteen months previously; there was a rumour doing the rounds that the joy riders were from this district. What he couldn't understand was why Stan Camac was bearing the brunt of Chaney, especially since he was inside at the time of Chaney's parent's death.

'Ye know something Gerry, you were always a good copper; not a callous bastard like that piece of shite on the floor. Me as well as a lot of others put you through a fair bit of crap but you took it. What I liked about you was if somebody said they didn't do it; you half believed them. 'See dat thing there soiling my ma's lino,' he nodded towards the battered and groaning form lying on the floor.' He used to kick the cunt out of everybody, even girls. Well now that I trust you, Gerry, I want you to look after my child, ok?' he whispered breathlessly. More tears started to stream down his face. Gerry McNiffe remained silent. Stan Camac's eyes said it all; they were bouncing around his head. He was manic. He had crossed the line.

'Promise me Gerry,' he pleaded.

'I promise, but why can't you look after your own child?' Gerry pleaded, realising the calmness had deserted his voice.

'Gerry, I'm straight mate. Like my fellow criminals I detest sex crimes. They're going to send me to the Hill, shame me; I can't live that way and therefore I really gotta go," he added. McNiffe's pleading and begging as he tried frantically to remove his bonds were to no avail. Thurstan 'Stan' Camac ended his life at the early age of twenty years. He jumped from the second story balcony of his mother's flat, impaling himself on the railings below. What would haunt Gerry Mc Niffe's dreams for a long, long time to come was that the young man never uttered a sound as he sailed over the balcony to his death.

The Green Mitten

Dora Areh

'I must hurry,' Geraldine said aloud as she swept into the grounds of the crèche. Finding a parking space several yards from the front door, she jammed on the brakes and sprang out of her little convertible. Office job complete, twins to collect, dinner to cook, an hour to study for the exam she was taking – choir practice at the church-meeting of the gardener's club. 'The green light is always on in my life,' she once remarked. ' No red light to stop me in my tracks.'

Halfway to the front door, she spied a little old lady hobbling along in front of her. She was wearing a grey woollen tracksuit, green mittens and a picture hat pulled down in front to shade her eyes and she carried a walking stick. As Geraldine approached she stopped, turned around and waited. Geraldine fancied she had seen that face before somewhere. The penetrating grey eyes seemed familiar but try as she might she could not remember where or when.

'Ah,' said the woman, ' I knew I'd find you here.'

'Pardon me,' replied the mystified Geraldine, 'do I know you?'

'O, yes. You know me,' rejoined the other, 'you're here to collect your twin girls and I to collect my twin boys.'

As far as Geraldine knew, hers were the only twins attending the crèche and, as there was a long waiting list, it was unlikely that new ones had been accepted.

'But..,' she began and then bit her lip, deciding the old lady was doting or, more technically, suffering from Alzheimer's disease or cerebral sclerosis.

'Ah, of course, I remember,' she said kindly, though she had little time to spare and felt considerable consternation when the old lady linked her arm and leaned heavily against her.

It was at the front door when Geraldine lifted her free hand to ring the bell that she became aware of a strange sensation in her head. It was a feeling quite new to her – neither dizziness nor pain. She seemed to be watching the rewinding of videotape. But strangest of all was her companion. The years had fallen away from her and she was clad in a light summer dress, fashionable in the early 1940s. Glancing down at herself she saw that her own tee shirt and jeans had been replaced by a dirndl skirt and blouse.

The location too had altered. This was not Dublin. It might be London or some other city in the south of wartime England. She could hear the fighter planes zooming overhead, the crack of the gunfire and a heavy thud in the distance causing the ground to tremble beneath her feet.

Instinctively she knew. This woman was working with her in the munitions' factory. They always came here together after work to collect their twins – her girls and the other woman's boys. There was a raid in progress and they must dive into the Anderson Shelter – that structure of corrugated iron fortified with sandbags that graced the back yard. It had been built as a protection against flying glass and shrapnel – thought nothing would save a body from a direct hit.

Geraldine pushed her way through the side gate then was bending to gain entrance into the shelter. Accustoming her eyes to the semi–darkness, she became aware of the silhouettes of the young children huddled together with the pinkies – young nursery assistants. Her own were among them – hers – but not Sarah and Imelda whose existence was now very vague.

As she stood trying to sort out the mixed thoughts that were running through her head, there came – very near to her – a deafening whistle followed by a thud so heavy that she felt herself falling forward. As she hit the ground, hazily, she wondered what became of Grace? Yes, that was the woman's name – Grace. She tried to open her mouth but no voice came – to lift her head, but it was like an immovable boulder. Everything and everyone around had stopped moving; it was a like silent tabloid. She felt faint. Her blood pressure was dropping.

After what seemed an eternity, her eyelids began to flicker and at last she was able to open them. Gradually she became conscious of solid figures moving around her and then she realised that she was sitting in an armchair in the office at the crèche where the senior nursery nurse was standing holding a glass of water to her lips.

Slowly her strength returned. 'Oh, you're back with us? You fainted out in the porch there. Maybe you're doing too much – common foible of this generation…' Geraldine remembered the old lady but something told her not to mention her.

Later when she was returning to her car with the twins, Sarah, the brightest of the two, spotted something on the ground. She pounced upon it and held it up to show her mother. Geraldine gasped as she recognised it as one of the green mittens worn by the old lady.

A Woman of Substance

Frank Callery

Albert. Thick as two short planks but glick enough to come in out of the rain or scream blue murder if he couldn't get his way. That's what she remembered now as she ran past Chancery House and onwards towards the bridge. Puffs of pride exhaled in her heavy breathing. Passing the flats always brought back scenes of the old life. The struggle, from fix to fix. The grind of life and the good neighbours in the same, sad bedlam. Dada and Mamma Irene and Albert and Patrick whom she had loved – all her former inmates on the top balcony; living from hand to mouth, from vein to vein.

Now she was running back to her new life, crossing the bridge, fording the old, dark river. She would soon be ascending the hill of the Winetaverners to the place where Christopher had died, to the new life with young Chris and his doting Effie. The evening sun was glinting on the granite of Adam and Eve's on Merchant's Quay as she approached. She blessed the bent quay and the place of her redemption. Saint Kilda's had opened a new path onto which her life had tumbled and begun to blossom again. In the five years since she had first trodden it, she had been remade in the image of her inner longing.

In a way, though, she thought, Albert was the lucky one. As long as he had food and drink and could wander around the markets picking up his bags of damaged fruit he hadn't a care in the world – unless the telly went or the St Vincent De Paul food parcel was shy of his six-pack of cans. 'Here's the Vinnies with the tinnies,' she remembered him screaming as he danced excitedly up and down the balcony in his filthy-runners. 'Adidas,' he had exclaimed to her once, 'the best, the best, the best!' running into the sparse and dirty flat. Sometimes in her delirium she had seen his feet running and screaming 'Adidas, Adidas,' as they bled and overspilled the lips of the gashed 'runners'. And later, when she herself had started to jog back to life, she would hear 'Adidas' or 'Abebe Bikila' ring in the hurt rhythms of her head. Abebe Bikila, the unshod, the grit of Roman streets printing his feet. A lone runner in the torch-lit black, like an old newsreel with Dada's voice-over – telling her 'I only saw him on the telly in the pub, but he was a splendid, brave man. Sacrificed though, punishing his body for our pleasure, and for what? A little bit of gold that was probably plundered from his own country in the first place.' 'Abebe' and 'Adidas' had remained constant through all the distances of her long runs.

Irene had known too well the chilled wastes and the deserts of the balcony; remembered the poverty and the smells; the infinity of its quick sands that still engrained her soul and her peace, scarifying her memories with its blatant abstract of pain. And here she was again, running through those lives and away from them. Away from the self she had once despised. The self that had clung, crying out to be hugged, like a child in a wet bed, the dark, tumbled world inured to its pain. Albert, her supposed halfwit brother, the only one left now in the dingy fiat; poor Patrick and Mamma Irene and Dada, all lost to pain and excess. She could still hear Mamma Irene exclaiming to her neighbours, one and all, as she tottered home from the pub: 'goodnight to yis all!' or 'good-fuckin-night!' Barging into the flat, looking for a tinnie, a singsong or a row. 'Come on Albert me little gobshite, give us "My Way"'. She could still hear him screaming as he ran into the bedroom with his arms about his head 'get away from me, get away from me, I fucking hate yis'. And Mamma singing

'Irene, Good Night, Irene' as she fell into her usual stupor. Once she had been the mainstay of the family; latterly the pathetic drunk among her junkie and dysfunctional offspring.

Mamma Irene had taken on Dada's mantle, holding, as he had, a well-read grudge reflected in the constantly hugged glass or the can. That was how she had come to picture Dada, an image reworked and imitative of her mother's bitter observation. He had been a cooper in the distillery until he was magically and suddenly 'let go'; he never worked again up to the day he died as an unwelcome resident in a night shelter. His little poems and plays had had glowing reviews in the family grate, to the singular applause of coal crackle and dry voucher-bought kindling and her mother's desolate sobs. Dada had spent many of his 'retirement' days in the nearby courts. He had even become a pub lackey for certain barristers who liked a drink. A barrack-room lawyer, telling them what Mr. Justice so-and-so would, and would not, tolerate. Recalling in minute detail the case of So-and-So versus So-and-So or as he liked to quip, 'the State versus Everybody'.

Irene had loved her Dada, shared his keen intelligence, his talent for drawing and the lore and the history of their native city. Once as they were looking at the paintings in Gerry Davis's window in Capel Street, a child in a pram, outside Fuscardi's Café, cried incessantly. When a woman emerged clutching a bag of chips, Dada said, 'Jasus, missus, will you pick that babby up and give it a bit of comfort.

'Its not my fucking pram, pick it up yourself.' He did, to Irene's embarrassment when the mother emerged and called him a 'Fucking baby snatcher!' They had walked, constantly, the familiar streets. Soaking in the history of its crumbling walls. Stepping out as if they possessed some magisterium, inspecting the nooks and crannies of falling buildings and blind alleys. Dog shit and child cry: smells and sounds and the drag of sun-drenched poverty.

Long walks were prefaced by: 'Come on, love, we'll ride the franchises today, reclaim the ould place for ourselves, huh'?

... and so forth on the high-way and leaving the stone well on the left-hand, they proceeded southward until they came into the high-way going to Ballyboght they came to the water of Tulkan by the bridge of Ballyboght, there passing over the water, keeping by the water-side southward, as far as they might ride, until they came unto St Mary's-abbey, leaving the abbey on the right hand. On the west of the abbey, on the wafer-side, there lyeth a stone...

'That's where they claim they buried poor Robert Emmet,' he had told her as they passed Saint Michan's and where, on the comer of May Lane, he dragged his long shadow into a public house while she stood outside drinking Taylor-Keith's lemonade and sucking an ice-pop. She had waited many times like this, absorbing the colours and sounds and the stresses of the city. Imbibing Dada's destructive inclinations. Returning as an abetter of his excuses to the mother she had loved as he had, a love that had never fully expressed itself. Now they were both dead and beyond reach, faint objects of momentary guilt and strange illusion.

Her mother, needily hard and off-hand – a firm defence to the tang of frequent poverty – always on the go, fetching and selling, reaping and robbing to feed her small brood, to keep warm the faint spark that occasionally flickered between herself and her 'man' until he finally doused all hope of togethemess and she, finally beaten, inherited his loss and his habits.

'A drink problem? We're the ones with the fucking drink problem,' she remembered the irony of her mother's scream at the curt enquiry of the social worker. 'His only problem is he can't get enough of the cursed stuff.' That scream had been as shrill as despair would allow. As shrill as the screams she could sometimes hear when she allowed the thoughts of her mother's dying to invade the small silences she tried, desperately, to arrange in her head. 'Oh Sweet Jesus, oh fuck, oh Mother Mary I'll never be gathered up.' The Capuchin from Church Street had stopped his ears against her peril as he held the claw of her hand, meekly; Irene's, almost wrenched from her drugged body by the other. And then the final silence that drove her out of her mother's singular misery, into her own. 'Carcinoma of the rising colon' written large by fountain pen, the ink, blue-black and blurred on the green certitude of that final statement.

While Albert processed his small, tight itinerary and Patrick thinned to a yellow-grey premature corpse, Irene had grown wayward in the white heat of her parents travail. She always seemed to take Dada's side, praising the seeming aplomb of his sayings: 'the wisdom of the ruined' he used to say with a self-regarding accuracy. He would feed her such titbits as:

'We are the boys of George's Hill,

We never worked and we never will.

Ours is not to reason why,

So fill your glass, and smoke, and die'

Once in George's Hill school she had changed the slang rhyme to:

'We are the girls of Georges Hill

We drink and smoke and we're on the pill'.

Sister Eustace had called her up but Irene denied authorship. 'A pity, Irene, I thought it rather an observant verse if not entirely immoral.' Irene assumed the shock she had anticipated in Sister Eustace. Being a bright and wayward pupil. Sister Eustace had wanted her to "mend her ways and to think strongly of taking the habit".

'You have a mind of great substance, great talents, Irene. Don't let them wither. Many people could benefit from them. Ours is not a bad life, Irene, we are fulfilled you know.'

Take the habit, take the pill. The choice made no demands for Irene and her friends. And through ignorance and being, as her mother put it: 'said and led by rossies and lousers', most of her school pals became unmarried mothers. Out of school and into childbirth, buggy-tied to a status symbol that would pain their lives, living in the shadows of the grimy neighbourhood in which old and young fathers were invisible or, at best, night visitors only. Irene had been held in school to finish her Leaving Cert, only by her mother's strength. 'Me daughter's the only one from the area to get eh,' she proudly and pathetically told her neighbours, who were none the wiser. Sister Eustace was. She praised Irene for 'sticking it out' in the face of all temptation.

'I suppose you wouldn't consider doing something else, Irene. I know NCAD is your first choice, and there is no doubting your talent, but I think you could do so much better if...' The echo of the slammed door and Irene's running footsteps receding down the corridor reverberated in Sister Eustace's head for a long time.

The Leaving got her into college and into trouble. Christopher became her life. They fed on each other and loved the intensity and the trauma of their creative and turbulent life. They were highly thought of at the National College of Art and Design. Two pupils who would someday make their name. His meticulous draughtsmanship, her infusive colour and imagery mingled in a fluent love and absorption that overrode the difference of social background and Effie's reservations. Effie loved her son with an unhealthy passion. A cosseted and pampered life, following his father's death, produced two Christophers, his mother's version and his own. 'This is Irene, mother, we are living together and she's expecting our child', he had said as he drew his mother's attention to his will, just as perfectly as he had drawn Irene's changing rotundity in their smoke-filled apartment, adding to each portrait as they both added to the small track marks on their beautiful young bodies.

Christopher died of an overdose of bad gear while Irene cried in the pangs of difficult birth. Young 'Chris', whom she named in memory of his dead father, bawled his painful way into a world of separation from Irene, and the over-indulgent love and custody of Effie. She, being good, and moneyed and a woman of substance in the community of Donnybrook, ensured that her grandson would have 'a chance in life'.He became 'a poor likkel mite' and 'Effie's likkel ba ba 'Kiss', a frequenter of at-home coffee mornings, Bridge and splendid gardens.

Irene floundered in and out of addiction, painting, doing the dreaded trade work for Ad agencies, relapsing, then trying to get clean and get custody of Chris. She and Effie had come painfully to an understanding and accommodation. Through Irene, Effie came to know of the real and other Christopher – becoming addicted to the need to know the son she thought she had known. At moments she resented 'this... 'this inner-city tramp's' possession of her son. In and through the constant rows and accusations,she came to know the drug habit she had unwittingly enabled; the covert estrangement her over-bearing love and misplaced generosity induced. And looking through the discarded portfolios of their work and Christopher's letters to Irene – from study trips he had made to galleries all over Europe – she slowly and honestly realised her place in the old and the new triumvirates of their lives. For a while, the reality of Irene's closeness to 'her' Christopher had hurt her, but time and truth forced themselves and in some notion of atonement she determined to befriend and help Irene. Irene would remain living in the apartment and see young Chris only when she was clean. Effie noticed the contents of the apartment mapping the ins and outs of Irene's habit and it was finally, with help from 'friends', that she got her placed on the recovery programme at Saint Kilda's.

The room had oppressed her. The people, the probing; these with their gentle, coercive tools: their feeler-gauges and soiled rags testing the unhinged emotions, mopping up the leakage and probing more. And these others too, having to bare their minds and shattered bodies to the shared needle of hope and the new reality.

Dada was constantly with her; their long walks through strange streets and unknowable cities. And the hand of Mamma Irene reaching to her from the balcony to pull her up and out of other sweats and her tremors, away from Patrick's thin grip which held her ankles in the sweaty vice of weightlessness. 'Irene good-night, Irene, Irene, good-night,' warbling from a hideous mouth and Albert, running, running, running, the endless tract of his circuits devoured by his dirty, sweaty runners.

It was Sister Eustace's voice that brought her from her reverie over the sketching pad.

'Irene, do you remember me?' For a moment she stared at the close-cropped hair and the smiling, radiant, lined face and smart casual clothes of the speaker.

'Sister Eustace,' she said, swallowing some gobbet of shame, 'what are you...'

'Simple enough, Irene, I work here, I run the programme, but I don't get to meet you until, well, you know, until you have been some way along the path, so to speak. But we are all here for the same reason.' Sister Eustace looked down at the pad to avert Irene's embarrassment.

'I see your talent has truly blossomed, as I once predicted it would. You have copied Sir lsumbras and the river brilliantly. Millais would be pleased, but I never took you for a Pre-Raphaelite!'

'Yes, I was... I was just doodling, you know, not wanting to have to think...'

'It's lovely', she said, turning to look at the print on the refectory wall, 'we find it an appropriate image for our house and our work, there is a sense of security in its..., shall I say, disproportion? A sense of crossing over.'

'Yes,' Irene said, knowingly, returning the smile her face had almost forgotten.

She felt the sweaty socks rub on her ankles as she gazed into the westering light suffusing Merchant's Quay. Dada was there, bestride the great black horse, the sun on his golden armour and ills, his strong arms enfolding. Mamma Irene stood on the further bank, waving and singing to them her evensong. Dada was older now and wiser as he bestrode the great flanks to ride out and lay claim to the franchise of their past and of their future; carrying her and little Chris where 'the water of Amliffy ' absorbed the old light and the new, and was now safely forded.

Portrait of Daddy

Marian Finlay

'I could write a book.' my mother would say when she had finished reminiscing about her youth, and I would be jerked back to reality, away from the picture evoked by my mother's words.

We are in the large flagged kitchen of Millpark with its enormous arch framing the open fire. In his special chair her grandfather, known affectionately as Daddy, sits smoking his pipe, my six-year-old mother standing by his knee. She is the baby of the family and his favourite. It is early afternoon. Both are watching the group of young people on the other side of the room beside the window, my mother's three older sisters, Mary and Sarah, who are in their teens, and Katy, two years older than my mother. Mary is darning a sock, and Sara is threading a string of coloured beads for Katy, while listening to the visitors, the two young men on whom her grandfather's gaze is fixed.

He takes no part in the conversation and feigns incomprehension when the visitors try to include him. The child knows that they are the Browne brothers, Dominic and Nicholas, sons of their former landlord, and although they are treated respectfully by her sisters, who always put the prefix Mister before their names when addressing them, she senses that her grandfather resents their presence. She also knows that her afternoon walk with her grandfather will be postponed 'til the young men have departed.

Daddy is guardian of his orphaned granddaughters and takes his responsibilities seriously.

Both visitors are wearing black arm-bands because they are in mourning for one of their brothers who has died recently, the second member of the family to die young. ' Consumption is in our family,' Mr Dominick is telling Sarah in his beautifully modulated voice. 'We are all at risk.' In his opinion all the misfortunes that have befallen this generation of his family are a punishment for the misdeeds of their ancestors and their harshness towards their tenants. Her grandfather grunts, and the brothers look suspiciously in his direction but his face remains impassive. She is too young to understand references to the Land Acts and Wyndham, but she realises that the Brownes were once rich and arrogant and no longer have any power.

Mr Dominick tries to include her grandfather in the conversation. 'Tell me, Patsy,' he asks courteously, 'how many years ago did you break your leg?' Grandfather stares blankly at him, pretending not to understand. He tries the question in Irish, laboriously struggling with a language that is foreign to him, and does not slip comfortably off his tongue. The sisters listen open-mouthed. 'Ce mheid blian,' he struggles with the unfamiliar words. 'Ce mheid blian o brokail tu do futty?' he finishes triumphantly. The old man, genuinely bewildered now, turns to Sarah and asks for an explanation. She translates rapidly. Grandfather turns away in disgust, spits into the fire and replies, 'Abair leis! Iarr ar mo thoin!' which Sarah, straight-faced, renders smoothly as 'He can't remember rightly, sir.' All maintain their composure.

The Brownes depart, but not before requesting once again if the old man will pose for his portrait, the real purpose of the visit. 'Such an interesting face and a wonderful profile!' Mr Nicholas enthuses. It will task all Sarah's inventiveness to frame the refusal in inoffensive language, but she implies that her grandfather would consider it unlucky to have his likeness transferred to canvas, and the brothers are too well-bred to pursue the matter.

The child runs to fetch Daddy's stick and hat and they set off on their daily walk towards the island, an acre of grass cut off from the surrounding bog by a stream that almost encircles it. This is the boundary between the Browne estate and Millpark. As they stroll along hand-in-hand he explains that the grass here is always greener than in the surrounding fields because it is holy ground where Mass was celebrated during the Penal days. He points out the stump of a dead tree where the sacred vessels were hidden from the authorities. She hangs on his every word.

In the distance she sees the large white house of the Browne family, a big house by local standards, but even with the later addition of an extra wing to accommodate the growing family, a relatively modest dwelling. Recalling the conversation in the kitchen she asks the old man to explain 'consumption' and he replies fiercely, 'The Brownes were bad! bad! and they'll melt like butter on a griddle.' There was a time, he informed her, when everybody had to bow and scrape when they met a member of the family. A lack of deference could lead to eviction. He cited an example. One of the sons owned a hunter and the stableboy, son of one of the tenants, was employed to groom the horse. Before the owner mounted he rubbed his silk handkerchief over the animal's flank and when he saw that the cloth was soiled he struck the groom across the shoulders with his riding crop. The youngster retaliated, and a bout of fisticuffs ensued. The gentleman was no match for the groom who gave him a terrible hiding.

'Of course he was sacked on the spot, and had to go to America.' Daddy told her. 'All the Mulrooneys were hot-headed, but that lad's quick temper left the long road under his foot. The family were lucky not to lose their holding.'

'Strange how the wheel turns!' my mother mused, 'all the Brownes of that generation ended up in America. They knew nothing about land and couldn't afford hired labour. The place went to rack and ruin. Mr Edward was the last of them. After his death the Land Commission took over the estate and striped the land among the tenants, but that's another story. Oh my God! Will you look at the time, and not a chore done!'

I realised that further chapters of the imaginary book would have to wait for another day. Now there were matters to be attended to, eggs to be collected, ducks to be rounded up before they absconded down the stream at the end of the garden and headed for the open lake, pails of fresh water to be replenished, and the log-basket filled for the night.

Meanwhile I was weaving my own version of the story, where in the best tradition of the romantic novels that I read surreptitiously, Mr Nicholas who was secretly in love with Sarah, followed her to America where he became a famous portrait painter, grew fabulously wealthy, married Sarah and they lived happily ever after.

'Did Sarah ever meet the Brownes in America?' I asked innocently one day when my Mother was once again in a talkative mood.

'She did, once only!'

I had already visualised the scene where Mr Nicholas, beautifully groomed and carrying a bunch of roses, arrived at Sara's door to declare his love. The real story as related by my mother was more prosaic and did not measure up to my romantic expectations.

'When Sarah was working as a parlourmaid in a mansion in Philadelphia the two brothers came to the door selling encyclopaedias. She knew them but they did not recognise her, and because they had come down in the world and were shabbily dressed she did not want to embarrass them. Her orders were to direct all travelling salesmen to the back-door, but she showed them into the reception room, and the lady of the house, realising they were well-bred, received them very graciously.'

I thought it strange that neither of the brothers recognised their old neighbour, but Mother thought that was understandable, because when Sarah came home on a holiday after five years in the States she had blossomed into such a beautiful girl that she bore no resemblance to the simple country girl she had been when she left home.

'And did Daddy ever pose for his portrait?'

My mother laughed: 'No fear! He wouldn't gratify the Brownes. Daddy had his pride too, and he thought that Mr Nicholas was trying to humiliate him. I'll never forget how angry he became when one of the Brownes suggested he should apply for the Old Age Pension. He associated the pension with Famine Relief, and flew into a rage, striking the ground with his stick and shouting, 'Níor ghlac mise Committee ariamh.' (I never took Committee.) 'That's what the old people called the money allocated by a committee to relieve distress among the poor in times of need,' she explained.

Apparently, Mr Nicholas was determined to get that portrait, so he set up his easel on his own land on the far side of the dividing stream and sketched the old man when he went for his daily walk. That was in 1908, the year before he died and before the Old Age Pension Act was passed. By then he had become so feeble that he had to pause for a long rest when he got to the Island before attempting the return journey, so without knowing it he struck the perfect pose. Daddy never saw the picture, and would have torn it up had he known of its existence, so to preserve the peace it was concealed behind a holy picture in the kitchen. All who saw it pronounced it a very good likeness.

'He didn't get the nose right,' my mother said, 'but when he tried to correct it he made it worse, and it was just a blob. I'm sure the portrait is still there in Millpark if they haven't got rid of the holy picture. I suppose I'm the only one alive now who remembers him,' she continued sadly, 'I loved that old man, and I was his pet.'

'Aunt Honor was so strict and she always said he had me spoilt.'

She would chuckle as she recalled how, when her aunt tried to punish her for some childish misdemeanour, she would hide behind his chair and he would threaten the irate aunt with his stick. When his corpse was laid out in the big bedroom she could not believe he was dead and sneaked in from time to time to check his breathing. She was surprised at how cold he was and could not understand why Aunt, who was such a skilful nurse, did not heat the bed.

Eventually, time caught up with Millpark. Despite many alterations the cosy dwelling that had survived the Night of the Big Wind of 1839 because of its sheltered position in the lee of the Hill field, became too cramped for the fifth generation of the family, and was replaced by a more modern dwelling nearer the main road. Mother was sad to see the abandonment of her old home. When asked if she wanted a souvenir she remembered Daddy's portrait, and a search through the accumulation of holy pictures from innumerable Missions revealed it.

I saw the slightly stooped figure of a very old man, with a pipe in his mouth, his hands clasped behind his back, his blackthorn stick tucked beneath his arm, dressed in the everyday clothes worn by country men in the closing years of the nineteenth century. It was all there, the hand-knitted, knee-length woollen stockings, the waistcoat over the bainin jacket, the caroline hat, even the unsuccessfully repaired nose, exactly as my mother had described it. In the distant background, barely visible, one could discern the outline of a small thatched house. Was this the original Millpark, as my great-grandfather had seen it when as a young man he had struggled home from a card-playing session on the night of the Big Wind? For me this was the closing chapter of my mother's unwritten book.